Sister Ruth Challis is amazed to find her cold heart melting towards untrustworthy consultant, Oliver Manning, but complications increase when her old friend Daniel's feelings about her become significant . . .

THE SISTER
AND
THE SURGEON

BY

LYNNE COLLINS

MILLS & BOON LIMITED
London . Sydney . Toronto

First published in Great Britain 1981
by Mills & Boon Limited, 15-16 Brook's Mews,
London W1

Australian copyright 1981
Philippine copyright 1981

ISBN 0 263 73640 7

Set in 10 on 11½ Times

Photoset by
Rowland Phototypesetting Ltd.,
Bury St. Edmunds, Suffolk.

Made and printed in Great Britain by Richard Clay
(The Chaucer Press) Ltd., Bungay, Suffolk.

CHAPTER ONE

Ruth stood at the window of her office that overlooked the hospital gardens, a very busy thoroughfare in the midst of the tall buildings. The statue of the founder, Sir Henry Hartlake, stood in the centre and seemed to be gazing with benevolent pride on the small group of student nurses from the Preliminary Training School who were taking a short break from lectures to bask in the warm sunshine.

They made a pretty picture in their blue check dresses with the puffed sleeves and matching belts, the tiny white caps with the one blue stripe of the first-year nurse. Hartlake had not adopted the national uniform like so many other teaching hospitals and its nurses felt that the distinctive garb was a precious part of a long tradition.

The students were all very young but it seemed to Ruth that they were much more sure of themselves than she had been when she first arrived at Hartlake. She smiled as she recalled those early days when she had been a very green junior, quite terrified at the thought of working on the wards and yet eager to be done with theory and textbooks and get on with the real business of nursing.

She had not really wanted to nurse. At eighteen, she had been very much in love and had little in mind but marriage, home and children. Neil was a medical student with not much money and a great deal of ambition. Both families had approved the engagement but pointed out that it might be years before they could afford to marry. In the meantime, Ruth ought to follow some kind of career.

It had been her mother's suggestion that she should train as a nurse and, with the thought in mind that she would make a better wife for a doctor if she knew something about his work, she had agreed, quite expecting to be married long before she finished the three-year course of training. For Neil was clever and highly-praised by his seniors and obviously destined to do well. In no time at all he would be qualified and able to marry her.

Almost absently, Ruth fingered the badge of the state registered nurse that was pinned to the bib of her apron. Fortunately, she enjoyed her work—and three years was quite long enough for anyone to get over the disappointment of being jilted, she told herself firmly. She had been reminded of the date by the desk calendar: the first of June, anniversary of what should have been her wedding-day. Having never found anyone to replace Neil in her life, it was probably very natural that she should feel a pang as the memories stirred.

No one could help falling out of love and she had forgiven him for that. It was also nice to know that he was doing so well. Only that morning she had seen his name in a national newspaper, one of the team who had carried out a heart transplant at the Central. There was high hopes for the patient but Ruth knew how swiftly those hopes could be dashed at the first signs of rejection.

6

Neil must be very pleased and proud she thought, with a little tenderness for the good-looking and very enthusiastic young man she had known and loved. She wished that she could tell him how delighted she was that he had been chosen to assist the internationally famous John Lindsay, pioneer in open-heart surgery and now leading the way in the still-controversial field of transplants. But he had not wished to see her again after that dreadful day when he had shattered all her dreams and, for a long time, Ruth had felt that she did not want to see him. It had helped that Neil had already left Hartlake for the more promising position at the Central.

She had almost left the hospital, too. It had been hard to face the well-meant sympathy of friends and colleagues, to know that the grapevine was buzzing with talk of her cancelled wedding plans. The first weeks had been very hard but she found that working to ease the pain and problems of the patients had helped her to forget her own.

Now she wore the dark-blue dress and high, frilled cap of a sister and ran her ward with quiet efficiency. She was not a martinet but she was very capable for all her youth, air of fragility and deceptively quiet manner. A slight, trim young woman with shining chestnut hair, whose curls she severely restrained in a neat chignon at the nape of her neck, and eyes that held more than a hint of green. She was usually regarded as a plain girl but her smile was very warm, very sweet, and turned her into a beauty without warning—it was known to brighten the dullest day and cheer the most depressed patient.

She had been in charge of Paterson, Women's Surgical, for nearly six months. She was liked and respected by her nurses for she was always fair and reasonable, always willing to listen, to make allowances, always prepared to work as hard as any junior on the ward when circumstances demanded and, in return, most of them worked just that little bit harder for Sister Challis.

She was roused from her reverie by a cheerful voice. "I've given Mrs Milsom her pre-med, Sister. Do you want me to go to Theatres with her?" Staff Nurse Jessica Brook came into the office, a pretty girl with a bright personality, an excellent nurse and a favourite with the patients. "She's still very nervous."

Ruth moved from the window. She ought not to be dreaming when there was work to be done. They were short-staffed that morning and if the ward was to be ready for consultants' rounds, she must help with some of the routine chores. She smiled at her staff nurse. "Sorry . . . I'm afraid I was day-dreaming. The cardinal sin on a busy ward!"

"I hope he's nice," Jessica teased lightly. Newly engaged, she was in that frame of mind when she wanted everyone to be as happy as she was herself but it troubled her just a little that the only man to interest Ruth Challis in years should have fallen headlong in love with her instead. She had not taken Lester away from Ruth, of course. They had never been anything more than friends. But she had broken up a beautiful friendship which might have been more with time. Ruth did not attract men very easily and the kind-hearted Jessica hoped that she had not been hurt by Lester's desertion. She liked Ruth, who had never shown jealousy or resentment and seemed genuinely pleased that she and Lester had found happiness after a somewhat stormy passage.

Ruth laughed. "I wasn't thinking about a man." She indicated the lively group of nurses in the gardens. "I've been remembering my own early days in P.T.S. . . . and how we all moaned and groaned and felt sure we'd never pass the prelim. and pretended that we didn't really want to be nurses, anyway. Those girls seem so carefree in comparison."

Jessica looked down at them. "They're just young," she said. "Too green to know what's in store for them, poor innocents. Sister Greaves never tired of telling us that it was all blood, sweat and tears. The new Sister Tutor is a sweetie, I'm told."

"They haven't got Sister Booth hanging over their heads, either," Ruth said with feeling, referring to an elderly dragon of a ward sister, now retired, whose rigid discipline and sharp tongue still lived in the memories of those who had incurred her wrath. Sister Booth had run her ward with a rod of iron and even the crustiest of consultants had occasionally bowed to her superior judgment and long experience. She had almost broken the hearts and the backs of her junior nurses but, looking back, Ruth and her colleagues knew that it had been excellent training for the days ahead.

"No, they've only got Sister Challis and she can be a devil when roused," Jessica said, tongue in cheek.

"It's time I *was* roused!" Ruth declared. "Just look at that clock! We shall have Oliver Manning and his swarm of students descending on us before we can turn round!"

Paterson was always a busy ward with its steady flow of surgical admissions, the almost daily preparation of patients for Theatres, the need for half-hourly observations on post-operatives, the continual call for nurses to 'special' the very ill—and, of course, the never-ending rounds that made up the daily routine of the ward. Drugs, pulse and temps., b.p.'s, dressings, bedpans and washings, fluid charts, bedmaking and back rubs, blanket baths, meals and drinks—so much work and so few hands to cope with it all, Ruth sometimes thought. But, somehow, almost miraculously it seemed at times, they did get through the work and the ward ran smoothly despite the occasional panic and the all-too-frequent emergency admissions.

Accompanied by a third-year nurse to check the dosage before giving it to the patients, Ruth went round with the drugs trolley which should never be left unlocked if they were both called away in the middle of the round.

She enjoyed this particular chore and usually liked to take her time over it if possible. It was a valuable opportunity to get to know the patients, to find out if they had any particular fear or anxiety, to learn about husbands or boy-friends and to encourage talk of children and grandchildren.

Domestic problems were usally much on the mind of women patients. If a woman was worrying about her husband's ability to run the home and do his job at the same time or wondering if the kids were running wild without her to keep an eye on them, she would take all the longer to get well.

Her warm smile and quietly reassuring manner made most patients feel that nothing was quite so bad or so frightening once it had been talked over with Sister Challis, who was so understanding and helpful.

She had almost finished the round when a stir of activity at the other end of the ward announced the arrival of the consultant for his teaching round. Ruth handed the keys of the drug trolley to Nurse Buckley and went to assist.

Oliver Manning was tall and lean and very attractive, dark of hair and eye—the kind of man who had an instant effect on impressionable patients and nurses. It was a long time since Ruth had been impressed for she had known him too long and too well. His smile was quite dazzling, she conceded, slow and very engaging, crinkling the dark eyes, causing most hearts to miss a beat. Its impact on her junior nurses usually meant that they were sighing and gossiping about him for far too long after he had completed his round and left the ward. Ruth felt that his smiling charm had won him too many foolish hearts throughout the years.

"Good morning, Mr Manning." Her tone was brisk, a little cool. Her smile swept over the group of medical students in their white coats. "You are a trifle early this morning."

"Not ready for me, Sister?" He was amused by the hint of rebuke. She seemed very young to take such a high tone with a senior consultant. Oliver found it difficult to take her seriously. At the same time, he had no fault to find with her work, her efficiency, her flair for organisation. She might be young but she was a splendid nurse. Destined to be Matron one day, no doubt.

"*Quite* ready, Mr Manning." There was just a hint of pride in the gentle rebuke. "Will you see Mrs Hobbs first? She is rather anxious to know the result of the tests."

Skilfully, she steered him towards the tidiest part of the ward while Jessica and a junior scurried to complete the remaining chores, another junior hastily retrieved a covered bedpan from a locker and vanished with it into the sluice and Nurse Buckley finished the drugs round at high speed.

The students trailed in the wake of the sister and the consultant surgeon, looking a little self-conscious and hoping that they exuded a general air of professional intelligence.

"I hope you enjoyed your holiday, Sister."

Ruth glanced up with a little smile. "Very much, thank you," she said primly but it was like him to remember that she had been away despite the fact that he was a very busy man with much on his mind. He had some very nice attributes if one chose to look for them, of course.

Oliver was amused by the impersonal coolness, so like her. She seemed to keep everyone at a slight distance, on and off duty, and particularly men. There had not been a murmur of gossip about Ruth Challis in all the years that he had known her. There had been an engagement at one time to a medical student but that had come to nothing and since then she seemed to have no interest in men. She was a dedicated nurse, apparently.

Oliver liked her because she was efficient without being full of starch. He liked her warm smile, her instinctive rapport with the patients, her swift grasp of a situation and her capable running of a busy and sometimes difficult ward. She knew how to delegate work to the best advantage and she got on well with her fellow-nurses. Her promotion to ward sister at a very early age had been generally well received, as well.

Mrs Hobbs eyed the tall consultant with some apprehension. He smiled at her reassuringly, took the chart from Ruth's hand and listened to her brief, verbal report. Then he turned to the patient. "I'm very glad to see you, my dear," he said for it had taken some persuasion to get the girl to come into hospital. "I've some

12

good news for you. All the tests indicate that only one ovary is seriously diseased and must come out. I hope we can get the other to function normally with the aid of a certain drug. If all goes well, you may be able to have the baby that you want, after all. We'll do our best for you, anyway."

The young woman, newly-married, hung on his every word, eyes large in her thin face. "Oh, Mr. Manning! Do you mean it? Oh, I am relieved!"

He patted her hand. "I'm sure you are. Now, if I may just examine you briefly and ask all the usual questions for the benefit of my colleagues. . ."

The students crowded round to look and listen attentively and to hope that they would have the right answer ready if a question was asked—a handful of young men and two very pretty girls.

Standing to one side, Ruth allowed her attention to wander. She was pleased for Mrs Hobbs who was so eager for a baby and had been so distressed by the thought of the operation which would effectively destroy all her hopes of motherhood. It was reassuring that Oliver Manning did not mean to whisk out both ovaries and be done with it. Obviously he could not guarantee that the treatment would be successful but it might just give the girl and her young husband the chance of parenthood.

His methods were sometimes unorthodox but they usually worked. He was very clever and very progressive and his recent appointment to a consultancy had been the reward for brilliant work in the field of surgery. He was very popular with patients—and not only for his looks and easy charm, Ruth admitted fairly. He was a genuinely caring man where his work was concerned and

13

was only callous when it came to dealing with the women in his life, she thought dryly.

He had been an assistant registrar when she began her training and seemed an almost god-like being to first-year nurses. She had been too much in love with Neil to bother about the handsome and reputedly amorous surgeon but the other girls in her set had promptly fallen in love with him. Only one of them had caught his fickle interest, to her cost. Prudence had belied her name and flouted all the rules for the sake of a tempestuous affair with a senior member of staff. She had left Hartlake in disgrace. Ruth had sympathised with her friend although it had been obvious that Oliver Manning was a shocking flirt who had only to lift a finger to have any woman he wanted . . . quite disastrous for a man who was much too handsome for anyone's good!

Ruth had disapproved of him because he was so obviously not the marrying kind. Clever and ambitious, working steadily towards a consultancy, he made no secret of his belief that a wife would be a drag on his career.

Now there was less talk of his affairs. Ruth fancied that he was more discreet rather than less busy in that direction. A consultant could not engage in casual affairs with junior nurses. The most recent rumour about Oliver Manning sprang from his attendance at Founder's Ball that year with Hilary Longhurst, the daughter of a hospital governor. An ambitious man needed to marry well and the girl was beautiful as well as wealthy and well-connected. There was speculation that the confirmed bachelor was beginning to have second thoughts about marriage.

Ruth wished the man would take a wife and turn

14

respectable. Then perhaps her juniors would spend less time dreaming about him and more time on their work, she thought, almost tartly.

The group of students fell back slightly and Oliver Manning moved away from the bed. Ruth paused to straighten the sheets and exchange a few words with the relieved and slightly euphoric Mrs Hobbs.

Oliver drew his students about him in the middle of the ward while he explained the history and the prognosis of his next patient, an eighty-four year old woman with a cancer of the womb. Despite her age, he had decided to do a hysterectomy and she was scheduled for Theatres that day.

Ruth hovered dutifully, trying not to seem impatient although a hundred and one things cried out for her attention. Tradition rather than necessity dictated her presence on the round. Some consultants thoughtfully released the ward sister or senior staff nurse so that she could carry on with her work. Oliver Manning obviously believed in involving the nursing staff as much as possible and certainly one could learn much from his examination and handling of patients, his quiet and authoritative explanation of a case to his students.

With a nod to Ruth to accompany him, he went to speak to the patient, signalling to the group of students to remain where they were as Miss Mallow would be alarmed by such a crowd. She was a little confused but wholly trusting, her rheumy old eyes never leaving his handsome face as he talked to her.

Ruth noticed that he held the old lady's hand gently in his own and that his smile was particularly warm. He sought to reasssure rather than to charm. She had seen him at work many times and was now wholly immune to

15

the attractiveness that seemed to bring other women low so easily. But she readily conceded that he had much to commend him professionally.

Oliver explained the operation in the simplest of terms and the gentlest of tones. Ruth stood by, ready to smile, to convey her own brand of reassurance, if Miss Mallow should look to her.

She became aware of Jessica at her elbow. "Yes, Staff. What is it?"

"Will you take a call, please, Sister? It's Mr Gold again—and he insists on speaking to you. He's rather upset."

Ruth stifled a sigh. It was the very difficult husband of one of her patients. He had complained about his wife's treatment from the first day of her admission to the ward. "Very well, Staff. Please take my place on the round." She murmured a word of excuse and slipped away. Oliver, quite engrossed with the old lady and intent on soothing her fears, scarcely noticed the substitution of one nurse for another.

Ruth was tactful but very firm with the irate Mr Gold who was now protesting that his wife wasn't fit enough for discharge and that he was not well himself and couldn't cope with a convalescent woman in a high-rise flat. Ruth's sympathy was all for the gentle Mrs Gold who had undergone a painful operation without one word of complaint and could not be glad to be going home to a bad-tempered husband who had behaved throughout as though her illness was a personal affront.

She replaced the receiver, thankful that they did not meet many such husbands. Most men were very grateful for all that was done for their wives.

The internal telephone buzzed. It was Theatres. A

patient was being returned to the ward from the recovery room. Ruth sent a first-year nurse for the patient and told another to prepare the side ward in readiness while she telephoned the office for an extra nurse to 'special'.

It was time to give an injection to a very ill patient. Then she showed a first-year nurse how to remove sutures. The post-operative coleostomy patient arrived on the ward and she helped a young houseman to set up a drip. Finally she caught up with some of the never-ending paperwork on her desk and even found time to add a few lines to her report.

She was glad of a break when a junior brought her tray of tea. She sipped it gratefully and glanced through the observation window in her office to notice the group of students slowly filtering from the ward. The round had been longer than usual and she was relieved that it was finished. Rounds were essential but they could be disruptive to the routine of the ward. The patients were unsettled and the younger nurses were distracted by a group of students, mostly men, moving about the ward. And, while she did not dislike Oliver Manning, she felt a little on the defensive whenever he was around. He was always pleasant to her, courteous and friendly but she could not rid herself of the odd conviction that those dark eyes saw far too much.

She had nothing to hide, of course. But it was disconcerting to feel that any man had the ability to look into one's mind—and, possibly, one's heart.

They met off the ward from time to time. On such social occasions, senior surgeons and consultants could be extremely stand-offish but Oliver Manning did not stand on his dignity with people he had worked with in earlier days at Hartlake. That, at least, was one of the nice things about him. Whenever they met socially, he did not forget that they had known each other, however casually, in the long-ago days when he was running around with Prudence and she was engaged to a medical student on his team. He took a polite interest in her health and her career and Ruth did not wish for anything more.

She was aware that she was not attractive to most men. She did not flirt and most of the men that she met were either young doctors with no time for serious involvement or patients who hoped to while away the boredom of convalescence.

She knew that she was not pretty and she realised that she was too serious-minded for the average man. Certainly she had never been to Oliver Manning's taste, she thought thankfully, remembering the heartache and humiliation suffered by Prudence who might have been a very good nurse if she had not fallen so foolishly in love with a heartless and much too attractive young surgeon.

It was something of a relief to Ruth that men like Oliver Manning respected her patent lack of interest in the casual flirtation that was indulged in by so many nurses—in many cases, a very necessary light relief to offset the long and arduous hours of work.

Ruth had worked very hard to get her own ward at such an early age. She had dedicated all her energies and enthusiasms to nursing. She felt that no man in the world could mean more to her and that marriage could never promise more satisfaction than she had found in her work. After all, she was a ward sister in a famous teaching hospital that had a long tradition and a world-wide reputation for high standards of nursing.

In her position, she felt that she could not afford to be

too friendly with any member of the staff, doctor or surgeon or medical student. For Hartlake adhered to old traditions and an old-fashioned code of conduct for its nurses.

CHAPTER TWO

Oliver paused by the open door of the office. He regarded the still figure for a moment or two, knowing that she was unaware of him. Unusually for Sister Challis, she seemed to be unaware of everything about her, lost in thought, tea cooling rapidly in the cup.

He had known her for a long time without really knowing her at all. In the early days, she had just been Prue's friend and when that affair came to an abrupt end he had felt that Ruth Challis blamed him and disapproved of him. He had been a little amused by the coolness in her attitude. Certainly, it had never entered his head to try to alter her opinion of him. She was an intense little thing, plain and uninspiring, not at all his type.

He recalled that he had not been very surprised when she was jilted by Neil Plummer. He had been more surprised by the engagement itself for she had seemed an unlikely bride for the light-hearted, lively young man with an eye for the girls. Ruth had seemed unaware that there *were* other girls in the man's life. No doubt she had been blinded by love, Oliver thought dryly, remembering the way she had looked at Plummer and the way she had hung on his every word. Much too intense. . . no man could live for long with that kind of idealistic adoration, however flattering. Plummer had obviously found it too much of a strain and backed away from the marriage before it was too late.

It was all some time ago now, of course. He knew nothing about Plummer except that he was doing well at the Central. Ruth had done well, too. She was very young to be a ward sister but had thrown herself into a nursing career with single-minded devotion and intensity of purpose just as she had obviously thrown herself into loving an unworthy young man. Hartlake had gained an excellent nurse. Plummer might have lost more than he knew. . .

Oliver knocked lightly on the open door of the office. "May I come in?"

Ruth was startled, disconcerted. She had supposed him to have left the ward with the students but she said swiftly: "Yes, of course . . .!" She capped her pen and smiled at him. "Do you mean to scold me for deserting the round? I had so much to do!"

Oliver had seen that smile before—the swift and rather sweet smile that illumined her gamine face and made it memorable. It could briefly dispel the belief that she was a plain young woman.

He had seen her angry, too: green eyes flashing, a heightened colour in the small face, words tumbling as she castigated a thoughtless lad in Accident and Emergency for bowling a wheelchair into an elderly patient just because he was bored and impatient with waiting for attention to a cut hand. She had shamed the boy into apology and then sent him for some tea for the shaken old man.

He had seen her alive with amused animation at a party, sparkling with enjoyment in the evening, green eyes dancing, a surprisingly witty tongue loosened by the wine, and wondered that he had always thought her of little interest. But, temporarily captivated by the girl who gave the party, he had turned away and forgotten that brief and unexpected stirring of attraction.

He had seen her intent on her work, carefully slipping a tube into place, a little frown in the green eyes, concentration giving a sharpness to the plain features—and then, task completed, genuine concern for the patient which softened and warmed that small and very ordinary face, giving it an unexpected bloom of beauty.

She was a chameleon, he had discovered, a little intrigued. Her face was so expressive, hinting at unsuspected depths for all the cool reserve of her manner. Sometimes he thought he would like to know more of her. But her attitude towards him was not encouraging and their paths seldom crossed outside the hospital walls.

"You provided me with an excellent substitute," he said lightly. "Nurse Brook, is it? Very capable. Much too pretty, though. Some of my students found it difficult to concentrate on my remarks." He gestured towards the tea-tray. "Would there be any tea left in that pot?"

"I'm afraid it isn't very fresh." She felt the sides of the pot. "We'll have some more . . ." She rose and went to the door to hail a passing junior. She was surprised that he was lingering on the ward. As a rule, he completed his round and left immediately.

Oliver's glance slid over the trim figure in the dark-blue dress. Her waist was so small that he fancied he could span it with his hands. Idly he wondered how she looked with that gleaming hair loosened and falling about her shoulders.

Ruth turned to find his dark eyes studying her intently. Her chin tilted just a fraction, quite unconsciously. Something that might have been amusement flickered in his gaze. "Won't you sit down . . .?" she said brightly. She felt that he was towering above her and she wished, not for the first time, that she was a little taller. Sometimes it was difficult to stand on one's dignity when one had to look up to a person.

Oliver shook his head. He turned to the window that overlooked the gardens, hands thrust into the pockets of his white coat. "I want to talk to you about Miss Mallow," he said, a little abruptly. "Some cause for concern there, don't you think?"

Ruth was foolishly relieved that he wished to discuss one of her patients. She wondered why she had supposed anything else when their relationship had always been so impersonal.

"She's very confused. I don't think she is quite aware of what is happening or why she is here," she agreed.

"Do you think I should operate?"

Ruth was surprised by the blunt question. It was not like Oliver Manning to doubt his own judgment—or to consult a ward sister in such matters.

"In view of her age, do you mean?"

"She's such a frail little lady," he mused. "I should be sorry to lose her on the table."

"Peter Armstrong seems to be quite happy about administering the anaesthetic," she said reassuringly. "He says that her heart and lungs are surprisingly sound."

"Yes, I know . . ." His tone was still doubtful.

Ruth hesitated. Then she said quietly: "By all accounts, she's a very active person with an amazing zest for life. It's only the drugs that have slowed her down and made her mentally confused. If you remove the condition that necessitates the drugs you may be giving her several more years of active and enjoyable life."

Oliver turned to look at her, thoughtful. "That's why I decided to do this hysterectomy. But today—I had the feeling that she would just slip away beneath my hands." He took his hands from his pockets and studied them . . . long-fingered, strong and muscular and extremely skilful hands that had been called upon to carry out the most delicate of operations.

"I think she has a tenacious hold on life," Ruth told him firmly. "She doesn't mean to be beaten by a mere cancer. And she trusts you, Oliver." She did not consciously use his first name. It slipped out, betraying the way she always thought of him. But they had known each other a long time and the correct formality of the ward did not have to be carried into the privacy of her little office.

Oliver smiled, warming to her. She was not flattering him with an empty compliment. The quiet words boosted his confidence. She obviously had faith in the power of an old lady's belief that he could cure what ailed her. Miracles could and did happen at Hartlake occasionally—and perhaps this was his day for one, he thought, spirits rising.

"I think she would like you to be present," he said lightly. "She trusts you, too."

"It isn't usual but I could certainly take her to Theatres if you wish," she suggested readily. "She'll be muzzy from the pre-med and may not even know me. But she might be pleased to know I was with her."

"Yes. Will you stay, Ruth? Scrub up and watch?" he asked unexpectedly. "I should appreciate it."

It was an unconventional request. Ruth was surprised

24

and just a little flattered despite her determination not to be swayed by his charm, his smooth tongue. She did not deceive herself that he was thinking of her as anything but a dedicated nurse who was keenly interested in a particular patient.

She knew his unorthodoxy. If he really felt that Miss Mallow stood a better chance of coming through an operation if she was present well, why not? She did not think it could make a scrap of difference to the outcome. But one made allowances for the fancies and foibles of a skilful and sensitive surgeon.

"I'd like that," she said, meaning it. "I don't often get the chance to watch you at work. We only see the end results on the ward."

"I must put on a really good performance for you," he said, smiling.

Nurse Fleming came into the room with the tray of fresh tea, ready to blush or giggle if the handsome consultant should smile or speak to her. But he did not even glance at her, she found to her chagrin. Standing by the window, he was smiling across the room at Sister Challis in a way that must mean something, she reported to her particular crony a few minutes later, and they spent a happy ten minutes speculating on the possibility of a romance between the sister and the surgeon.

Ruth poured tea for him, knowing just how he liked it—no sugar, very little milk. She had the kind of memory that retained such small but pleasing details.

Oliver observed and admired her economy of movement which was the sign of a well-trained nurse. She was restful, too. While they talked, she did not fidget with the papers on her desk, pick up and put down a pen, smooth her hair, toy with her teaspoon. She was quite relaxed, entirely at her ease. If her mind was on the neglected paperwork or the patients or the nurses who might or might not be carrying out their work efficiently while he monopolised her attention, she did not allow it to show.

There was not the smallest hint of coquetry in her manner, such as he found in most women. He was intrigued, interested. He did not even know if she liked him at all, he thought. She did not seem to respond to him as other women did. Those guarded green eyes gave very little away.

He had a busy day in front of him, patients waiting to see him, a long list to get through in Theatres, a dozen letters to dictate to his medical secretary. But he lingered, enjoying his tea, snatching a few minutes to relax in the company of a girl he knew only slightly and perhaps should get to know rather better.

He set his empty cup on the tray and rose to his feet. "I suppose I must get on." He smiled at her. "I know it's short notice, Ruth, but would you have dinner with me tonight?"

The invitation was unexpected and unwelcome. Her first instinct was to refuse. Whatever his motives, she had no wish to be talked about as Oliver Manning's newest flirt—and she did not doubt that the grapevine would be busy if she were to accept that surprising invitation. "I'm sorry. . ."

"I should like it very much," he said quietly. "I hope you would, too."

His smile was very warm, very engaging. Ruth had always understood why most women responded so readily to him. Fortunately, she had always been immune to his charm. Dark men were not much to her liking. Neil was very blond, almost Nordic—fair hair, fair skin, very blue eyes. So was Daniel, but no one at Hartlake knew about Daniel. Her private life was very much her own these days.

"I have another engagement, I'm afraid." She saw no need to explain further. He would not wish to know that she was going to see a cousin who had been confined to a wheelchair since a car crash two years before. Why should Oliver Manning be interested in Daniel whom he did not know?

"Quite impossible to cancel, I suppose?" He was not in the habit of coaxing a woman into going out with him. It had never been necessary, he thought dryly—and wondered why he persisted now in the face of obvious indifference.

She was a nice girl but not really his type, after all. And yet he was intrigued by the cool composure which might be only a mask for the fire and passion beneath. That hair, those green eyes, that tempting little body was all a waste if she was truly as frigid as she seemed. There was no such thing as a frigid woman, of course. Unawakened was the word for someone like Ruth Challis and he was tempted to find out if he could dispel the distrust of his sex that was the obvious legacy of her broken engagement.

Ruth looked at him, oddly torn. Daniel would certainly understand if she telephoned, excused herself. But he would be disappointed. And surely she did not really wish to spend the evening with Oliver Manning! "You would be very bored," she said slowly, knowing there was a world of difference between herself and the kind of woman he usually squired.

Oliver smiled. "I don't think so," he said firmly. She

would be a very pleasant change to the girls who usually filled his leisure hours, he felt. "I'll call for you at eight o'clock."

He was gone on the confident words, giving her no chance to demur. Ruth half-rose, meaning to hurry after him and deny that acceptance had been implied by her attitude. Then she sank back in her chair. He had taken swift advantage of her hesitation, interpreting it to his own satisfaction. Why had she hesitated, felt tempted? She did not trust Oliver Manning and she had never quite forgiven him for hurting Prue, for behaving so badly towards her friend. Such a man was best kept at a safe distance, she had always felt. And it was not wise for any nurse to become involved, however briefly or light-heartedly, with a senior member of the staff. The grapevine would be much too busy with unlikely rumours if she was to be seen in the consultant's company.

Daniel was expecting her, too. She was very fond of the man who accepted his disability so bravely and so cheerfully, knowing that he would never walk again. They were the best of friends. She could talk to Daniel, enjoy his company, confide in him—and he was perhaps the only man she could ever trust since Neil had let her down so badly.

When she met Oliver Manning that afternoon in Theatres, she would tell him quite frankly that she had no intention of going out with him that night or any other . . .

Theatre Sister was an old friend and readily agreed to the suggestion that Ruth should be present during the hysterectomy on Miss Mallow. She donned the green surgical gown and boots and scrubbed up with meticu-

28

lous care. Oliver came into the ante-room and nodded to her briefly, his mind already on his work. Miss Mallow was on the table and in Peter Armstrong's capable hands and he was waiting for the anaesthetist to give him the signal to begin the operation.

Ruth thought Oliver looked weary, a little anxious. Miss Mallow was the last of a long list and he had been operating steadily all the afternoon. No doubt he was tired. She wondered if he was also apprehensive. A surgeon had to be supremely confident in his skill but a sensitive surgeon sometimes had the intuitive feeling that he would lose his patient on the table—and sometimes he was right. It happened only on rare occasions and Ruth sent up a silent prayer that the frail little woman would survive the operation and return to the ward. If they lost her from post-operative shock or complications, not too unexpected with regard to her age, then Oliver need not feel that he had done anything but his best.

"She's going to be all right," she told him quietly.

Oliver looked at the slight figure in the surgical green, not really registering her identity or the words. He had forgotten his apprehension. Just now, the patient was someone who needed his skill, his sensitivity, his ability to cure with the knife. He knew exactly what to do and how to do it and he did not doubt that the operation would be successful. Later, the patient would be well again, or not. No one could predict with certainty when a patient was so advanced in years. He would do his best as always—and leave the rest to the gods.

Ruth was fascinated by the swiftness and the sureness of the surgeon's hands. No wonder the gallery was always filled to capacity with students who wished to learn from this clever man. His technique was almost breathtaking. She had heard so much about his work and there was little opportunity for her to observe it in general. She was usually only concerned with the after-care of his patients and she knew that he had many successes to his credit. He would often go in where other surgeons hesitated and he had been known to take chances. But his unorthodox methods seemed to work, she thought with instinctive admiration.

At last Oliver stepped back from the table. "She'll do, I think," he said with quiet satisfaction.

He peeled off his surgical gloves and discarded them. He drew down his mask and smiled at Ruth who had supposed him to be completely unaware of her presence throughout the operation. She felt a little glow of warmth as at a shared sense of relief.

The anaesthetist was busy with his complicated machine, the cylinders of gas and oxygen, and very soon Miss Mallow was wheeled into the recovery room and the theatre staff began to tidy up, thankful to have reached the end of the list.

"She came through it well," Peter Armstrong commented. "Marvellous constitution some of these old ladies have, you know. The eighty year olds of that generation are survivors—and no doubt they had to be when one remembers the conditions of their childhood!"

"Tough as old boots," agreed Roger Pelling, the registrar who had assisted. "But so stubborn! She should have gone to her G.P. long before she did, of course. Why won't these old biddies admit to being ill now that they don't have to worry about paying the doctor's bill?"

"Sometimes it's domestic anxiety. . . a husband who can't be left because he's more frail and totally depen-

30

dent. The worry about who'll feed the cat or the dog. Sometimes it's common or garden fear of having a suspicion confirmed. . . and they don't have to be old for that," Ruth volunteered from her considerable experience of patients who had neglected their health.

"Now come along, lads. Haven't you homes to go to? We want to see the back of you as soon as possible," roundly declared Theatre Sister, bustling into the room. Liz Carter was a plump, jolly girl who treated all the surgeons like schoolboys from the most junior house surgeon to the most senior consultant. "You must have better things to do than to stand here gossiping!"

Hurriedly the men vanished into the surgeons' changing room to divest themselves of boots and gowns. Before leaving Theatres, Ruth went into the recovery room to check Miss Mallow's condition. Soon she would be returned to the ward and the capable care of the night nursing staff. There did not appear to be any complications, any cause for concern.

Walking home to her tiny flat just a stone's throw from the hospital, Ruth realised that she had not cancelled her arrangement to dine with Oliver. Theatres had scarcely seemed the right surroundings for personal matters.

In all the years that she had known him, they had been casual acquaintances, no more. She wondered what had prompted him to put their relationship on a friendlier footing suddenly. Perhaps he had already regretted that impulsive invitation. But he would probably turn up on her doorstep at the appointed time and so she must telephone Daniel as soon as she got in.

Oliver joined his registrar for a drink in the pub across the road, a favourite haunt of Hartlake staff. He might be a consultant but he saw no reason to stand on ceremony with members of his team when the day's work was done.

Relaxing, he was content to listen rather than talk and Roger was obligingly garrulous. Oliver was tired, looking forward to putting work behind him for a few hours. He ran a hand across his eyes, pinched the bridge of his nose to ease a slight pressure. The arc lights in Theatres could weary the eyes which had to be constantly vigilant for the smallest sign of trouble.

Two staff nurses were at a nearby table and Roger drew his attention to the girls, hinting that they might be congenial companions for the evening. Oliver was reminded of his date with Ruth Challis and he wondered if he was in the mood for her quiet intensity, her single-minded seriousness. A man wanted a little amusement after a day's work, to make love to a pretty girl . . .

One of the nurses caught his eye and smiled with a hint of invitation. They knew each other slightly. Oliver smiled back, almost tempted, trying to remember her name but having not the least difficulty in remembering how she had melted against him when they danced at a recent party.

Ruth had not wanted to go out with him. He had virtually forced her hand, in fact. Perhaps he should have left well alone for she did not really attract him and he fancied that she had always disapproved of him. But he could not go back on their arrangement. He was not that kind of man.

He left Roger making a beeline for the two nurses and collected his car from its usual parking space. He knew where Ruth lived. He had dropped her off occasionally after a party or a late hospital dinner. She had drifted in and out of his life for years without making much impression on it, in fact.

His car drew smoothly to a halt outside the tall, rather shabby house in a narrow street not far from the hospital. He paused on the pavement, tall and lean and very attractive in the dark grey suit, his crisp dark hair worn just a little long, the dark eyes crinkling in a swift smile for a nurse he recognised as she came out of the house. She smiled a little uncertainly and hurried off to keep a date of her own. Oliver looked for Ruth's name among the cluster of bell-pushes. The big old house was home to more than he had realised.

It was exactly eight o'clock.

Torn between wanting to go and not wanting to go, Ruth's heart jumped at the sound of the doorbell. She stared at her reflection in the mirror. She felt very plain—and was sure that she looked it. The floral silk dress was a mistake, she realised too late. It was very fashionable but it did not suit her—perhaps she should have worn something else.

She had allowed her bright chestnut hair to tumble in deep waves and curls about her face—and had then hastily swept it into the usual knot because she could not be pretty if she tried and there was no point in trying for Oliver who had known her too long.

The bell rang again with a hint of male impatience. Ruth caught up a coat and checked that she had purse and keys in her bag.

She descended the narrow stairway, heart thumping with nervous apprehension rather than any anticipation in the pleasure of the evening. She did not really want to go out with a man that she was not too sure she liked. Daniel had been disappointed, too, and her explanation had sounded very lame in her own ears.

33

CHAPTER THREE

Oliver turned as the door opened.

He smiled at her warmly. Ruth smiled back, a little doubtfully, a guarded expression in her green eyes. She knew his reputation and did not mean to be too encouraging even if it was unlikely that he was in serious pursuit.

Oliver's glance took in the careful make-up, the shining hair, the fashionable dress. She had taken pains to please him just like any woman and he felt a slight compunction, wondering if his manner had misled her. She was not sought-after much by men, he suspected, and his invitation might have raised her hopes. Then he reminded himself that she was not a junior nurse, just out of school, head filled with romantic nonsense. Ruth was a grown woman, level-headed, mature and very sensible—and her experience in the past had probably taught her to hang on to her heart.

"You're ready—and you look charming," he said approvingly.

"Thank you. . ." Ruth was stiff, doubting his sincerity, distrusting the easy manner, the confident smile, the hint of intimacy in the touch of his hand at her elbow as they descended the stone steps.

Sitting beside him in the luxurious car, she felt absurdly shy. He was not a stranger but she did not really know him, she realised. The very casualness of their relationship in the past was a barrier to the new intimacy he sought, for whatever reason.

She stole a glance at the handsome profile and thought he looked stern but perhaps he was just bored and regretting the waste of an evening. She forced herself to make polite and rather empty conversation and fancied that his answering tone was as stilted as her own.

Oliver sensed her constraint. He hoped the evening would not prove to be a disaster. Earlier in the day, he had thought her attractive in the dark-blue dress, slender and appealing. He knew that when she was animated, she could look almost beautiful but now she was cold, almost unapproachable, keeping him at a distance with the rather brittle remarks that she might make to a stranger at a party.

He was not disappointed because he did not know what he had hoped for when he issued that impulsive invitation. But he was intrigued—and he wondered if that seeming coldness could turn into glowing, passionate fire if a man went about it the right way.

Desire stirred for he was a sensual man and responded instinctively to such a challenge. But he realised that it could take weeks or even months to persuade someone as wary as Ruth into bed—and he did not welcome the degree of involvement that might be demanded of him. He liked and enjoyed his freedom too much.

He suspected that she was the type of girl who would feel that loving was necessary to an intimate relationship. Well, he could coax her into loving him, he thought with all the confidence of a man who had never failed to win any woman he wanted. But she might love too much, give too much—and suffer too much when he walked away at the end of the affair. She had been hurt before. . . and he liked her too much to hurt her again, he thought wryly.

It seemed almost a pity. But perhaps it would be wise to make this evening together the first and the last.

He took her to a little restaurant in Soho and Ruth liked it immediately. She looked about her with glowing interest, deciding humorously that the subdued lighting could only be flattering to her and would certainly tone down the much-too-vivid colouring of her dress. Oliver looked particularly attractive, a slight harshness in his features softened by the mellow lamplight, and she was thankful that she had never been at all susceptible to his good looks, his engaging smile.

It might be possible to like him more than she had expected but there was no fear of becoming emotionally involved with him. He was just not the type to appeal to her—and he was much too dark, anyway. She only liked fair men, she thought, with a sudden pang of wistful recollection. It was still the first of June and it was impossible to forget all that day had meant in her life.

"What do you think?" he asked, studying the swift play of expression across the small face.

She smiled at him. "Nice . . ."

"You haven't been here before?"

She shook her head. "No. Is it one of your favourite places?" Had he brought many of his women here, she wondered, well aware of his busy love life. Suddenly the suspicion crossed her mind that he regarded her as a possible conquest. She doubted it—but one never knew with a man like Oliver Manning. However, he was certainly doomed to disappointment if he did have any hopes in that direction, she thought firmly.

The food and the wine were excellent. Music played softly in the background. Ruth relaxed and began to enjoy herself and discovered that he could be very good company. They talked of Hartlake, cases past and present, mutual friends. They went on to talk of books and music, films and the theatre, and found that they had several tastes in common. Ruth ceased to be shy and became quite animated.

Oliver ordered more wine.

They danced and he did not make the mistake of holding her too close. He discovered that her body was a delight to hold. Desire stirred once more as the faint perfume of her hair teased his nostrils. "We must do this again," he murmured, his lips close to her ear.

Ruth's hand tightened slightly on his shoulder. "Why not . . .?" she agreed, a little recklessly. She looked up, smiling. "It's fun."

"Not much fun in your life, is there?" he said gently, perceptively.

She stiffened. "I wouldn't say that."

"You're much too serious for a girl of your age. Your life seems to be all work. But there's more to living than striving to be Matron, surely?"

"I've no wish to be Matron," she returned truthfully. "I'm happy as I am."

He looked into the small, set face and blundered on. "You could be a lot happier."

"Oh? What's your recipe for happiness?" she asked tartly. "Men, I suppose."

He smiled. "A great many girls are thinking of marriage at your age."

The pain she had been suppressing all day suddenly

welled to the surface. "And a great many men are running away from it," she said bitterly. She drew herself from his arms. "Mind if we sit down? A nurse's feet are not at their best on the dance floor. I've trodden on you twice."

Oliver followed her back to their table, cursing his thoughtlessness. When they were seated, he tentatively covered her slim hand with his own. "Sorry . . . that was tactless, wasn't it?"

She moved her hand to pick up her glass of wine, sipped it. "I don't know why you are suddenly so concerned."

He poured more wine into his own glass. He had hurt her with that clumsy reminder of the past. "You work so hard and you care so much," he said quietly, warmly. "Who cares about you, Ruth?"

Her heart gave an odd little jolt as she met the warmth in his dark eyes. But she did not deceive herself that he felt anything more than an unexpected and quite unnecessary compassion. "I'm not without friends," she said brightly. "You don't have to be sorry for me, Oliver." It was oddly depressing to discover just why he had taken her out that evening.

He moved impatiently. She misunderstood his concern. "You live alone in that bloody awful place . . ."

"By choice!" she said quickly. "I've tried sharing. I didn't like it."

"You work all the hours God sends . . ."

"We're short-staffed!" Her tone was crisp. "I'm needed."

"When do you ever go out, enjoy yourself?" he demanded.

Her chin tilted. "Frequently!"

He leaned forward, intent. "A nice girl like you should have someone special in her life. Nursing can't be enough."

"There is someone," she said, proud.

Oliver checked, looked his surprise. "I didn't know. . ."

"Obviously."

He smiled at her warmly. "Well, I'm glad. But you keep your secrets well. The grapevine usually knows these things."

"I keep my private life well away from Hartlake these days," she said coolly. "The gossips had a merry time with my affairs in the past. It won't happen again."

He regarded her thoughtfully. "Do you ever see or hear anything of Neil Plummer?"

"I don't see him. I hear news of him from time to time. So do you, I daresay," she added shrewdly. "There was some mention of him in the *Mail* this morning . . . he was one of the team who carried out the latest transplant at the Central. I expect you read about it." She was pleased that she could talk of Neil so easily to this man who knew just how shattered she had been to lose him.

"People were talking about it," he agreed.

She looked at him steadily. "It was nice of you to think of cheering me up, Oliver. But it wasn't necessary, you see. I got over Neil a very long time ago."

"I didn't ask you out to cheer you up," he said lightly. "I knew you were too sensible to be still fretting over that worthless young man."

She winced inwardly at his careless dismissal of the Neil who had been so dear to her. "Why *did* you ask me?"

39

He shrugged. "No particular reason except that I thought it would be pleasant to be with you . . . and it is. We've been friends for a long time, Ruth. I like you," he said easily.

A little colour crept into her small face. She looked down at her plate. "I don't think we've ever been friends, exactly," she reminded him honestly.

He smiled. "You didn't like me at all in the early days," he recalled. "I think the shadow of Prue coloured your opinion of me to a very great extent."

She glanced up. "You were rotten to her!"

He raised an amused eyebrow. "My dear girl! I didn't father her wretched infant," he protested. "I'm afraid you didn't know your friend as well as you supposed. I was not the only man in her life."

"She was in love with you," Ruth said quietly.

"Perhaps. It happens," he drawled.

She looked at him with dislike. "Too often!"

A little smile played about his lips. "The grapevine has had a busy time with my affairs, too," he commented dryly. "But you mustn't believe all you hear, Ruth. I'm not quite as black as I'm painted."

"I don't know why I should blame you," she said with wry impatience. "The silly girls throw themselves at you. I've seen it time and again."

"It's an occupational hazard," he declared lightly, amused by her vehemence.

She threw him a sceptical glance. "Part of the perks, you mean!"

Oliver laughed. "Not for a consultant! I have to turn a blind eye to the prettiest junior these days. Fortunately, I may still be seen about with an attractive Sister without outraging etiquette."

She ignored the compliment. "Or the daughter of a hospital governor."

"Yes, indeed. The lovely Hilary." His eyes twinkled. "One's private life is just not one's own," he sighed.

"Not when one parades it at Founder's Ball, certainly," Ruth agreed dryly.

He leaned forward. "I would rather have danced all night with you—even if you do tread on my toes!"

She smiled, a little doubtfully, not believing him. He was too much of a charmer, too glib. She was immune to the attraction of those dancing dark eyes, the handsome face, the warm smile and the meaningful touch of his hand. Yet her heart could quicken now and again, she admitted honestly, and she had experienced a foolish little melting of the senses when she danced with him, an involuntary response to his physical magnetism. She was glad that he was not in serious pursuit of her for she might have been just as tempted to give in to the magic of the moment as any of those silly girls who had fallen victim to his charm in the past.

"Time we were going, I think," she said, glancing at her watch. It was astonishing how quickly the time had passed in his company. But perhaps it had dragged for him. He was much too nice to show the boredom that he might be feeling.

The merest hint of the personal and she backed away, Oliver thought ruefully. Because she did not trust him in the slightest, or because of that 'someone special' in her life? He had been really surprised by her claim to have found a substitute for her former love. For deep in those green eyes was a little pain, a little sadness, a hurt not yet healed. And she was wary, distant, distrustful. Perhaps it was true enough that she had found someone to care

41

for her. But he doubted if she had yet learned to love again.

He did not want the evening to end. He had enjoyed her company so much more than he had thought possible. He liked her. He liked the smile that dawned in those expressive eyes and swept across the small face to transform her with surprising beauty. He liked to listen to her speaking—the soft, lilting voice was enchanting with its hint of country music and she could converse on a variety of subjects with intelligence and her own brand of philosophy. He liked her moments of stillness when she wrapped herself in her thoughts, withdrew from him—and the contrasting quickness of wit and laughter and youthful eagerness when she forgot to be shy with him. He liked the unassuming modesty and the sweetness and the warmth that he had never suspected. It touched him to see her surprise when he convinced her with the right word or the right expression in his eyes that he was really enjoying her company. He wondered at the stupidity and the blindness that had kept him from enjoying it before.

She was a sensitive girl who had been dealt a bad blow by a man she loved and trusted. It had wounded her pride, diminished her confidence and hurt her heart. A woman in love did not recover too easily from that kind of hurt and humiliation. Without conceit, Oliver felt that he could have helped if he had taken the trouble. He had always liked her, quite instinctively. But she had not liked him and never trusted him because of that brief affair with her friend. Perhaps he had been a little hurt, slightly offended, by her readiness to think ill of him. However, he had ignored the occasional tug of interest and attraction—and now it was probably too late to discover how much he liked her and how strongly she stirred his sensuality with those intriguing green eyes and that swift, sweet smile.

He took her hand as they walked along the brightly-lit pavements of Soho towards his parked car. She turned her head to smile at him and his heart contracted, quite unexpectedly.

He told himself sharply not to be a bloody fool. He'd been in and out of love a dozen times, never seriously. Surely he wasn't losing his head over a plain little Puritan he'd known for years! He merely fancied her, he decided. The slender waist, the narrow hips, the tilting little breasts turned him on . . . and her lack of response to him challenged the charm and the expertise that had won him any woman he wanted in the past.

He had been hesitating all evening about taking matters further. She was the type to take a man's attentions too seriously and he did not have serious involvement in mind. But now he knew that he wanted her too much to walk away and he was determined to break through the reserve and the resistance that he sensed in her.

Driving her home through almost-deserted streets, he said lightly: "This 'someone special' that you mentioned . . . does he have a name?"

She was comfortable, deliciously drowsy from the warmth of the car and the unaccustomed wine. She could not immediately make sense of what he'd said. Then she recalled that moment of pride and the foolish seizing on Daniel's affection for her. Well, he was fond of her and she suspected that his life had begun to revolve about her visits. They were cousins but that would be no bar to marriage if he should ask and she chose to consent for there could not be any children. The terrible car crash had left Daniel incapable of being a husband in anything but name.

"Daniel . . . Daniel Seaton."

"He means a lot to you, does he?" His tone was deceptively casual.

"I'm very fond of him," Ruth agreed. "We're cousins so I've known him all my life."

"And you grew up with Neil Plummer?"

Ruth was surprised that he remembered—or that he had even known. She did not think he had taken much interest in her engagement to Neil—and it was a long time ago. "More or less. His mother went to school with my mother. Neil and I were matched in our cradles." And had failed to fulfil that sentimental wish of their families. Her mother had never forgiven Neil. His mother had laid the blame at her door. So old friends had quarrelled and never spoken to each other again.

"You seem to cling to the familiar," Oliver said dryly. "The family friend—and now a cousin."

She coloured faintly. "I don't make friends very easily."

"Oh, nonsense! We're friends, aren't we? Did you find it so difficult?" he demanded, teasing.

She smiled at him, reassured by his light tone. "No, of course not."

"Yes, you did," he corrected, smiling. "It's taken years to get you to go out with me."

She eyed him with scepticism. "It's taken you that long to work your way down the list!"

"I believe in keeping the best until last," Oliver returned, dark eyes twinkling.

She shook her head at him reproachfully. He laughed and stretched out a hand to touch her own. His touch

44

sent a little tingling shock down her spine. She did not move her hand but she wondered if it was wise to leave it beneath his clasp. While she dithered, he brought the car to a halt and she realised that she was home.

She discovered that her heart was hammering. Would he merely wish her goodnight in a casual manner—or would he kiss her? And did she want him to kiss her? One kiss would certainly alter the entire fabric of their relationship, she knew. But it had changed from the moment that he issued his invitation. The easy impersonality could never be recaptured after the pleasant intimacy of the evening she had spent with him. She had seen another side of him—and liked it. She had been a little drawn by his physical magnetism, a little captivated by his charm. Most important of all, liking for him had crystallised. They were friends for the first time in all the years that she had known him and she very much wanted his friendship, his liking.

Daniel was a dear and she was fond of him but he was rapidly becoming dependent upon her. Ruth had no one to lean on. Sometimes a girl needed a shoulder, some friendly adviser, a supporter so that she need not feel she was battling on her own against the world. Sometimes a girl needed to feel that she was attractive, too, a desirable woman and not just an efficient cog in the very big wheel that was Hartlake Hospital.

Whether or not he meant it or simply could not help flirting with anything in skirts, Oliver made her feel that she was a woman—and a friend.

"Come in for coffee," she invited airily as though she were in the habit of asking men up to her flat after midnight.

Oliver was amused. She was trying so hard to be the

woman of the world, he thought—and it was obvious that she was terrified he would begin to make love to her. He suspected that she was utterly inexperienced and doubted if she would know how to cope with his advances if they were not welcome. He felt the ache of desire but did not mean to rush his fences where she was concerned. She must be coaxed into his arms . . .

He wandered about the small sitting-room, studying her books, her pictures, the one or two good pieces of porcelain. He skimmed through the pile of records and placed one on the turntable.

Ruth came out of the tiny kitchen with two mugs. "Oliver! One o'clock in the morning!" she protested as music filled the room.

He lowered the volume until it was just a gentle background. "I suppose these walls are made of cardboard."

"Just about." She handed him a mug. "I hope it's how you like it . . ."

"Perfect." He set it down untasted and sat on the couch, stretching his long legs. "How long have you lived here, Ruth?"

"Two years." She glanced at him, smiling. "You don't approve."

He shrugged. "None of my business. But you could do better than this, you know."

"It's convenient and the rent isn't too exorbitant and I can talk 'shop' with my neighbours at any hour of the day or night . . . this place is virtually an extension of the Nurses' Home." Ruth perched on the arm of the couch, sipping her coffee. His dark head was level with her shoulder. She felt the impulse to touch a hand to the crisp, gleaming waves, the tiny curls that nestled at the nape of his neck. She tightened both hands about the

46

mug, her heart beating too fast. The treacherous body that had not reacted to any man for over three years was clamouring with sudden urgency in response to his nearness.

It was the wine, the unusual excitement of an evening out with an attractive man, the new and not too welcome awareness of his physical magnetism. It had been a mistake to invite him up, she decided, hoping he did not sense that foolish turmoil in her blood.

There was no hint of amorous intent in his manner. Ruth should have been reassured but, instead, she was humiliated. She was not at all attractive to him, obviously. He felt no desire to kiss her, to embrace her. His motive for taking her out had been nothing but kindness and, horrible thought, perhaps a certain pity for a jilted girl that no other man had apparently ever wanted.

Perhaps there was something wrong with her. Perhaps she did not stir any man to physical desire. Neil had never seemed to mind her touch-me-not insistence that they should wait for marriage—and he had not married her, in the end. Because she left him cold, she wondered, rather late in the day. Daniel had never shown any particular interest in her until the accident that had robbed him of his manhood yet before it he had chased the girls with the best of them. Not her, of course, because they were cousins and because of Neil. Or was it because he had simply not found her physically attractive?

Now, Oliver, a notorious womaniser with a string of conquests to his credit, sat in her flat while the rest of the world slept, talking of music, popular and classic, giving not the least indication that she appealed to him as a woman.

It was a relief, of course.

She could have cried with disappointment and the terrible feeling of rejection . . .

CHAPTER FOUR

Oliver leaned his head back on the cushion and closed his eyes. It had been a long day. He was near to sleeping in that quiet room with the murmur of music in the background. Ruth, curled cosily in an armchair, was very restful company. They had talked and listened to music that they both loved and he had forgotten the lateness of the hour, the fact that another busy day beckoned for them both.

Now he suddenly realised his weariness. He thought that he would like to lay his head on her breast and sleep, her arms about him. He reined his wandering fancy, wryly amused. He did not usually have sleep in mind when he held a girl in his arms. He must be more tired than he knew!

He looked at his watch and decided that it was too late to drive halfway across London to his flat. He would return to the hospital, look in on Miss Mallow on Paterson and spend what was left of the night on the comfortable couch in his office, not for the first time.

He said as much, lightly, rising to his feet, stretching his tall body, smiling at her with lazy warmth.

"You could stay if you like." She kept her tone very matter of fact. "A couple of pillows and a blanket turns that sofa into a reasonably comfortable bed."

The woman of the world touch again, he thought, a

little moved. She was so anxious to prove that she was no prude in today's permissive society. But the faint blush of colour in her face and a shy reluctance to meet his eyes told its own story. He did not think that many men, if any, had spent the night on Ruth's sofa . . . or in her bed!

"I'm flattered that you'd risk your reputation for my sake," he teased gently. "But it won't do, Sister Challis. Just think what Matron would say!"

"No one would know . . ." She broke off, remembering that his very distinctive car was parked outside the house. All her neighbours were Hartlake nurses and the fact that he had stayed the night would be all over the hospital in the twinkling of an eye. It was quite impossible to have a private life or even to enjoy a wholly innocent friendship with a man who was known to the entire staff of the hospital as a womaniser.

"Unless I told them?" His eyes narrowed, hardened. "You really don't think much of me, do you?"

"Oh, Oliver! Don't be silly," she said firmly. "I was thinking about your car. It is a trifle conspicuous, you know!"

He relaxed, laughed. "Very true." His dark eyes were suddenly warm, teasing. "There are times when you put me in mind of Sister Booth—and this is one of them!"

"I suspect that isn't a compliment," Ruth returned dryly. She picked up the mugs and placed them on the tray. She felt a little pang at the thought that one day she might seem an elderly martinet to a succession of juniors. She loved nursing. It had been the purpose and the fulfilment that she needed during the last three years. But did she really want to devote her entire life to Hartlake? Did she have a choice?

It was not difficult to feel that she was singularly unattractive in the eyes of any normal, healthy male. Oliver had spent more than an hour with her and treated her like a sister. Suddenly depressed, she picked up the tray and carried it into the kitchen. She ran the tap and rinsed the mugs.

Oliver stood in the doorway, watching the neat, methodical movements. Those slim hands were so capable, so deft—and he had seen them at work very often, carrying out much more delicate and skilful tasks.

Now, she kept him at a slight distance with the domestic busyness. Was she apprehensive—or just cold? It was impossible to know, he thought wryly, unless he made the first move towards a more intimate relationship, yet it was still too soon, too tricky, where Ruth was concerned. One wrong word, one wrong move, and he would fail before he had even begun to coax her into surrender.

"Thanks for the coffee."

She turned to smile. "Thanks for a lovely dinner." She reached for a teacloth, dried her hands. He was going with just a casual word, a careless ease—and she would be glad to be alone, to slip between the sheets of her lonely bed, to forget all about him in that world of dreams where a man did not hurt or disappoint or reject so pointedly.

"We'll do it again."

"Yes . . ." Ruth knew how little importance she should attach to that light assurance. If a man wished to repeat an experience, then he spoke of times and places, she thought wearily.

She was not encouraging. Her attitude implied a total lack of interest in him as friend or lover, Oliver felt.

51

Earlier, it had seemed a spur. Now he wondered if it was worth making the effort to win her trust and affection.

At the door of the flat, they shook hands. Ruth thanked him again for a pleasant evening in a cool little voice—and then impulsively reached up to brush his lean cheek with her lips. The formal parting was much too cold-blooded when they had known each other so long, she told herself, justifying that sudden and rather foolish impulse.

Oliver turned away and began to descend the stairs as quietly as he could in consideration for the sleeping occupants of the old house. Ruth waited at the head of the stairs until he closed the heavy front door behind him. Then, with an oddly heavy heart, she went back into her flat.

She did not know what she had expected. She told herself that he was used to women throwing themselves at him. She desperately regretted that impulsive kiss and comforted herself with the belief that he had scarcely noticed it. Which did not comfort her at all!

She closed the door, stood with her back to it, troubled. It was a long time since her emotions had been in such turmoil and she did not want to find herself wanting Oliver Manning when he was just being kind.

She recalled some of the girls who had flitted in and out of his life and marvelled that she would suppose even for a moment that he found her attractive. It was only too obvious that his interest was no more than friendly, entirely platonic. She must not make the mistake of becoming too intense where he was concerned, she told herself firmly.

She had loved Neil too much—and no doubt that was just one of the reasons why she had lost him. A man did not feel comfortable with a woman who set him on a pedestal for he knew that he could not live up to her shining ideal. She had loved him too much—and he had discovered just in time that he did not love her enough.

No one knew just how greatly her confidence had been shaken by that unexpected change of heart. She had never doubted that Neil loved her or that they would eventually marry. All her plans for the future had revolved about him and nursing had been only a temporary interest until their marriage.

The date had been fixed and invitations sent out, her wedding dress bought and presents beginning to arrive, most of the arrangements finalised—there were only a few weeks left before she would be Neil's wife when she suddenly found herself without him and with no apparent future but nursing.

For some time she had been desperately unhappy, wondering how and where she had failed and why he no longer loved her. She had continued with her training because she found comfort in the calm impersonality of hospital surroundings, in being needed by the patients, and she had thrown herself heart and soul into her work, needing a new purpose for her life. Her fellow-nurses had been too busy to take more than a passing interest in her broken engagement and she had been allowed to forget it to some extent.

The wound was not entirely healed even now but losing Neil had not been the end of the world, after all. It had made a difference to her life and her outlook, of course. Nursing had become all-important. She felt that she really mattered to someone who was ill or in pain or anxious or despairing. She was useful, she was needed and it was encouraging to feel that she was generally liked and trusted by the patients. It always brought a welcome lift to her heart to return to a ward after a spell off-duty to discover that she had been missed.

But there was more to life than job satisfaction and there were times when Ruth felt very lonely and envied her junior nurses their busy social lives, their light-hearted flirtations. She was still young despite the dark-blue dress and sister's cap and it seemed very hard that she should miss out on so much just because Neil had failed to live up to all her youthful dreams of him. At the same time, she was certainly not reduced to throwing herself at a man like Oliver Manning, she told herself sternly, and determined to be very cool and off-putting when they next met just in case he should imagine that she was interested in him.

Oliver slid behind the wheel of his car but did not immediately turn the key in the ignition. He touched a hand to his cheek where her lips had brushed, still rather shaken. It had been an unexpected gesture—but he had already discovered that there were hidden depths to the quiet Sister Challis. He suspected that the demure and rather distant manner was just a cloak for the warm and generous nature of a girl who had learned to guard her heart since it had been thrown back at her so cruelly.

He was suddenly reluctant to let Ruth slip through his fingers. He wanted her very much. He was glad that his instinct had held him back from making love to her with the casual ease that had characterised his affairs in the past. Ruth was not like the previous women in his life and it was essential that he should treat her differently. She was not the type to be picked up and then dropped as the fancy took him. She did not take life and love as lightly as most girls of her age. She was too sensitive, too vulnerable, too cautious—although she had shown that she could be impulsive.

If he wanted her, he might have to commit himself more than ever before. Unless he was prepared to give up the freedom that had always meant so much to him, then he must call a halt now, before it was too late, before he found himself really in love for the first time in his life.

The next morning, Ruth hurried into the ward and along to her office with brisk steps. Not surprisingly, she had overslept and for the first time that she could recall, she was late on duty.

Jessica Brook had coped in her absence and Ruth thought how much she would miss the capable staff nurse when she left to marry Lester Thorn.

Ruth had always liked Lester. He was one of the very few men she had dated in recent years, occasionally meeting him for a drink in the *Kingfisher*, sometimes going out for a meal or to a party with him. It had been a friendly relationship without sentiment on either side. Even the grapevine had found nothing to interest it in the casual association between the surgical registrar and herself, she thought dryly.

Lester had fallen headlong in love with Jessica. It had taken him a long time to convince her that her happiness could only be found with him and Jessica had even become engaged to another man, causing Lester to leave Hartlake for a research post at the Central.

Ruth was delighted that the romance had had a happy ending but she could not help a pang of envy whenever she saw the glowing happiness in Jessica's lovely face and listened to the rapturous account of wedding plans.

Fortunately, there was no time this morning for confidences. Ruth took a clean apron from the cupboard and pinned it on, symbol of being on duty. "I'm afraid I'm rather late," she said briskly. "Any crises?" She sat down at the desk and glanced over night sister's report.

"An emergency appendectomy admitted just before breakfast. Mr Gold took his wife home under protest. Mrs Hobbs is running a temperature and her op has been postponed for tests to see if she's reacting to drugs or picked up a bug. And Miss Mallow died in the night." Jessica leaned to point out the relevant remarks on the report.

Ruth stared at the neat script, dismayed. "I'm very sorry," she said and meant it.

"She seemed to be doing well," Jessica said. "She was being carefully observed . . . pulse, b.p., drip, drainage tubes checked every half hour. She was awake and quite comfortable and surprisingly alert when Mr Manning saw her . . ."

"Mr Manning?" Ruth looked up quickly. So he had carried out that intention of seeing the old lady. He had not admitted to concern, just a natural interest. She was glad that he had seen and spoken to the patient, but was sad that Miss Mallow should have died and wondered if he felt that he should have allowed the cancer to take its course.

"It isn't in the report," Jessica pointed out. "I heard it from Nurse Grant. He came in about two this morning and sat with the old lady for some time. They talked a little and then she went to sleep, holding his hand. She had gone when a nurse went in ten minutes later to check the drip . . . a peaceful passing, no trouble to anyone."

"In death as in life," Ruth murmured.

"Was Mr Manning personally interested, Sister?"

Curiosity touched the girl's voice. "Not every consultant would take so much trouble."

"I don't believe he knew her except as a patient. Now, what about arrangements?" Ruth asked crisply. "Has anything been done? She had no family, I believe."

"Pamela Bristow has everything in hand." Jessica referred to one of the social workers who acted as liaison between the hospital and the elderly of the immediate district.

"Good. I'll have a word with her later." She would attend the funeral, Ruth decided, representing the hospital that had done its best for the old lady and representing herself because she had liked and admired Miss Mallow. "Will you check the drugs trolley for stock while I make a start on some of this paperwork, please, Staff. And I'd love some tea if one of the juniors could find time to make it. I skipped breakfast."

"Late night, Sister?" Jessica smiled warmly.

"Oh dear . . . does it show?" Ruth ran her fingers over the faint smudges beneath her eyes. She had not slept at all until first light—and then slept too heavily and had woke unrefreshed. "That will teach me to lead a fast life!"

Jessica laughed at such an unlikelihood and went away. Ruth rose and went to the window and opened it wide. It was a lovely day, sun very bright in a cloudless blue sky. June weather—a day for the country or the coast, a day for patients to be irritable and restless, chafing against enforced confinement when the rest of the world was free to enjoy itself.

She looked down at the gardens, such a busy thoroughfare with its constant stream of people taking a short cut from one part of the hospital to another . . .

patients and relatives, nurses and students and porters, physiotherapists and radiographers and auxiliary staff, the occasional ambulanceman. Here and there people paused to speak, to smile, to ask a question or just to breathe in the summer air before plunging once more into the labrynth of wards and corridors, departments and kitchens, laboratories and more wards.

She looked down at the gardens but did not really see the familiar scene. She had a vivid mental picture of a surgical team working so skilfully to save a life. Particularly, she saw the concentration in a pair of dark eyes, the beads of sweat on a tired brow, the swift expertise of sensitive, muscular hands and she heard again the little sigh of satisfaction with a job well done.

It had been an advanced cancer and Miss Mallow would have died very soon, anyway. But did Oliver feel that he had precipitated the old lady's death?

He operated only two days a week at Hartlake. This was not one of his days for Theatres. But she knew he took a clinic that morning and wondered if he would find a moment to visit the ward to speak to her—and then asked herself if it was likely. He was a busy man with much on his mind. Miss Mallow had only been one of many patients . . . and in the hospital world one soon discovered that it was a very transient one. Patients came and patients went for one reason or another. There was always a new problem, a new interest, a new success or failure to take the place of the old.

She did not see Oliver and wisely did not spend too much time thinking about him. Mrs Hobbs was found to have an infection of the urinary tract and was instantly removed to a side-ward. Ruth had to organise and supervise a great deal of disinfecting and scrubbing and sterilising to eradicate the danger of cross-infection. Antibiotics soon made the young woman feel much better but the necessary delay in carrying out the operation which she had dreaded led her to talk of discharging herself. Ruth had to be very firm with her—and wondered if she really was becoming as fierce and as feared as the legendary Sister Booth!

She was off-duty that afternoon and decided to take a bus to Woodford where Daniel lived with his family. He would be pleased to see her and she might be able to shake off the persistent thoughts of Oliver Manning.

Daniel did not like seeing her in uniform as it reminded him too much of the long and traumatic months he had spent in hospital. So she dressed in a summer suit of apple green linen and a pretty green, yellow and white shirt. Waiting at the bus stop, she looked so cool and fresh despite the shimmering heat of the day that she attracted several admiring glances, but noticed none of them.

Nor did she see the gleaming silver car with its personalised number plate until it drew smoothly to a halt beside the queue of people at the bus stop. There were so many cars.

Oliver leaned across to open the passenger door, called her name. "Where are you going?" He had finished his clinic, lunched with another consultant before leaving the hospital and only the merest chance had brought him along the High Street and caused him to glance at the waiting line of people as the busy traffic almost brought his car to a standstill.

Ruth demurred instinctively. "A long way . . . Woodford!"

"Get in." She still hesitated. "Come on!" He was

impatient, his glance going to the driving mirror where he could see the approach of one of London's red double-decker buses, trundling towards the stop.

Ruth scrambled into the car beside him, conscious that people were staring. "Thank you—but surely it will take you well out of your way?"

"Not at all," he said smoothly. He smiled at her and set the car in motion just as the bus reached the stop. "I'm going to see a private patient in that part of the world," he told her without truth.

Ruth had no reason to doubt him. She relaxed and smiled. "Then I'm grateful. Usually I take the train but it involves a long walk at the other end. The bus does drop me at the corner of my cousin's turning but the service isn't too reliable, I'm afraid."

The heavy stream of traffic took much of his attention but he glanced at her, eyes narrowing. She looked almost pretty, the bright sun finding all the gold in her chestnut hair, green eyes sparkling and a little colour in her cheeks which he attributed to anticipation and excitement. "Cousin Daniel, I assume?" he asked lightly.

"Yes."

"Regular trek, is it? By bus or train?"

She was a little puzzled by his interest. "I try to see him at least once a week. He looks forward so much to my visits."

He raised a slightly mocking eyebrow. "All the way to Woodford after a day on the ward—and by public transport. Greater love hath no woman," he said dryly, marvelling at how much this woman would do to please the man in her life.

Her chin tilted. "Love doesn't come into it!"

"No?" He smiled. "You shouldn't spoil him, you

know. You should make him come to see you on your home ground."

"You don't understand," she said quickly. "Daniel is a paraplegic. He injured his spine in a car crash a couple of years ago."

"I see . . ." he said slowly. And suddenly he did see—much more than she knew. "I'm sorry. Poor devil . . ."

"He's an artist so it isn't as bad as it might have been. He does a lot of commercial work, advertisements and book illustrations and that kind of thing—free-lance, of course. It makes him financially independent and that means a lot to a man."

They were held up by traffic lights. Oliver smiled at her with sudden warmth. "I daresay your visits mean a lot, too. You're a nice girl, Ruth."

She was pleased, slightly embarrassed. "I'm very fond of Daniel," she said quietly.

"So it isn't just an errand of mercy?"

"He doesn't need that kind of sympathy," she said, a little sharp. She added firmly: "I *like* to see him."

The lights changed and Oliver drove on, wrestling with a vague uneasiness. After a moment or two, he said merely: "You must direct me when we get to Gates Corner."

It seemed to Ruth that the luxurious car covered the distance almost too quickly. She enjoyed the drive and thought how surprised and envious some of her junior nurses would be if they could see her with Oliver Manning in his silver Rolls Royce. It surprised her, too, she thought wryly. In all the years they had never been on such easy terms.

Perhaps it was the sunshine, the lovely day. Perhaps it

was just a sudden, selfish urge to get as far away as possible from sickness and suffering. But she found herself wishing that they could drive on, eating up the miles, until they reached the coast and there walk along the water's edge, enjoying the sea and the sun.

She caught up her thoughts. She was going to see Daniel, who relied so much on her visits, and Oliver had a duty to the patient he was going to see that afternoon. They could not just forget everything and everybody for the sake of their own pleasure and she had no reason to suppose that her company would be such a delight to him, anyway.

She did not know why she hankered so much for the company of a man she had never particularly liked through the years. Perhaps she was just being foolish, feeling flattered by his sudden and quite inexplicable interest after all the years of casual indifference.

CHAPTER FIVE

Sylvia Seaton was on her knees in the front garden, weeding a flower bed, a shabby old straw hat dragged over straggly grey hair as protection against the afternoon sun. As the impressive car glided to a halt outside the house she glanced up, first curious and then astonished as she saw her niece beside the driver. She got to her feet, a little stiffly, and went to the gate.

Ruth introduced Oliver to her aunt with a little reluctance that she could not analyse. Then she thanked him again and he drove away. She watched the car as it moved slowly along the tree-lined avenue and then she turned, linking her hand in her aunt's arm. "How are you, Aunt Sylvia?"

"Perfectly well, dear. But I don't like this heat," she said absently, still looking after the departing car. She was a little troubled by the implications of Ruth's arrival in the expensive car driven by a handsome stranger. "That's a very attractive man," she said, a little disapprovingly.

Ruth smiled. "Isn't he?" Then she relented for she was fond of her aunt. "He's one of our consultants. He had to come to Woodford to see a patient and kindly offered me a lift. How's Daniel?"

"Well, he was very low when you didn't come last night. He looks forward so much to seeing you." There

63

was just a hint of gentle reproach behind the words. "He's in the studio, of course. But he won't mind being interrupted by you, dear. Why don't you go and talk to him while I just finish off this flower bed and then I'll make us all some tea."

Obediently Ruth went around the house to the brick-built extension that served as studio and living quarters for her disabled cousin. Daniel would not say anything about her failure to turn up on the previous evening, she knew. He did not make demands on her. But her aunt's words confirmed the growing suspicion that he was becoming very dependent on her visits and, perhaps, on her affection and support.

He was a big, fair man. The very blue eyes and the silky blond beard gave him the look of a handsome viking.

Despite the wheelchair, the useless legs and the impotent body, he gave the impression of great strength and virility and a lusty enjoyment of life. He had been a devil-may-care and a practical joker, a man's man who played a lot of rugger and drank a lot of beer and enjoyed a lot of women. Driving back from a rugger match and the subsequent drinking bout with his friends, he had overturned his car on a motorway. After some months of deep depression, he had come to terms with the loss of his physical activity and salvaged his career from the debris of his life. By working from home he had achieved considerable success as a free-lance commercial artist, for he was clever and determined.

He was currently working on a series of advertisements in cartoon form for a brand of beer—and a couple of empty cans near at hand testified to his belief in the product.

He turned his head at the sound of Ruth's step, his eyes lighting up. Throwing down his pencil, he steered his motorised chair towards her, a warm welcome in his smile for the girl who had become of so much importance in his life. He was more than fond of her. He needed her desperately. He wanted to marry her but any man in his position knew that it was impossible to ask a woman to share his restricted way of life.

He had so little to offer. Even his love could not be expressed in a physical manner, he thought without bitterness, having long accepted that the sexuality which had once been so much a part of his life belonged to the past. At one time, he had felt that he might as well have died with his two friends in that horrific car crash. But he had begun to find many compensations despite the terrible burden of guilt—and Ruth's warm affection, tender concern and frequent thought for him was one of the most valuable to him.

"Ruth! This is a surprise!" he said gladly.

She bent to kiss him—the easy, natural token of affection that she always bestowed on him, unaware of its effect on his heart. His large hand briefly cradled the bright head. The touch was so familiar, so undisturbing, that she scarcely realised the love or the tenderness in the caress.

"I hope I'm not disturbing a genius at work," she said lightly.

"To hell with work. I'd much rather talk to you!" He jerked his head towards the open patio doors. "Shall we go out into the garden? It won't be too hot for you? Although I must say you look cool enough for someone who has walked all the way from the station in this heat!"

"I didn't come by train today." Ruth sat in a chair on the paved terrace that was surrounded by beautiful, heavily scented roses. She knew that his mother would mention Oliver and his car if she did not. "A friend brought me by car. I was very grateful, too."

"Man friend?"

His tone was teasing but she caught the hint of sharpness behind the words. It was probably natural enough that he should feel an occasional resentment of an able-bodied man who could do all the things he had once enjoyed so much—drive a car, chat up the girls, live life to the full. But he did not need to be jealous of Oliver, she thought confidently. He was not in serious pursuit. He was not even flirting. He was just being friendly. For some reason, rather late in the day, he wished her to know that there was a nicer side to him. But while she liked him more now than at any time in their acquaintance, she did not mean to like him too much.

"Why, yes . . . and a consultant, no less," she said brightly. "Oliver Manning, in fact. You must have heard me speak of him." She wondered if there was just a little consciousness in her voice. Daniel was sensitive to the slightest nuance.

He frowned. "I thought you didn't like him."

She talked a great deal about Hartlake, the patients, members of the staff. He had a good memory for names. He always listened with particular care when she spoke of doctors or surgeons with whom she worked. Oliver Manning was a name he knew. It conjured up an immediate picture of a man who was clever and successful and attractive to women. He remembered that Ruth had spoken slightingly of him in the past. But women were unpredictable and she might have suddenly decided to like the man—particularly if he was taking a flattering interest in her at last.

Until his accident, Daniel had felt only a casual affection for the girl who was his cousin. He had never thought of her as a woman. Sexually, his taste had always run to the flamboyant, the vividly attractive, the light of heart like himself. But the sexual urge had died with the lower part of his body and he looked for very different qualities in a woman than her physical attractions, her sensuality, her experience as a lover.

His love for Ruth had grown so gradually that, for some time, he had not recognised the feeling for what it was. It was not the kind of loving he had known in the past which had been sexually-motivated. His feeling for Ruth transcended the physical. There had been time and opportunity to realise her warmth and sweetness and integrity, her natural generosity of heart and spirit, her swift and loving concern for others.

She had become very precious. Her happiness was all-important to him. He loved her very much and he wanted with all his heart to spend the rest of his life with her. But it was his sincere hope that she would find a man to love her, to give her everything that she deserved, to offer her a normal marriage and the joys of motherhood—the right of every woman.

So it was not jealousy of an unknown man that stirred at her words but concern. For she was so gentle and trusting and she did not know men as he did—he was instinctively suspicious of the Oliver Mannings of this world. Like himself, a man could take a long time to realise that Ruth was enchantingly unlike other girls and that she was much too innocent for her own good. She probably would not believe that Manning only regarded her as a sexual conquest until it was too late and he wondered how to warn her against encouraging the man.

Ruth smiled reassuringly. "He was coming to this area and it would have been foolish to refuse the offer of a lift. Anyway, I don't dislike him. I just don't know him very well as a person. Surgeons, and particularly consultants, can be very remote creatures, you know." She reached for his hand and squeezed it. "Don't frown at me, Daniel. He isn't interested in me. I'm not his type."

"For some men, any woman is the type," Daniel said dryly.

Ruth laughed. "For some surgeons, anything in a nurse's uniform is just a robot trained to carry out instructions. We aren't women at all!"

"That isn't uniform," Daniel pointed out, his glance approving the summery elegance of suit and shirt and high-heeled sandals.

"He didn't notice, believe me." Her tone was almost wry.

She hoped that Daniel was not going to exaggerate a very ordinary incident out of all proportion. She knew that his life revolved around her very much these days. She knew that she was the only woman in his life now and that he needed her. She realised that he had a great deal of time in which to think, to brood, to plan a future in which she played an important part and to dwell on the fear of losing her to another man who could give her more than he could.

Sometimes Ruth toyed with the idea of marrying him. She knew it was often in his mind. They were the best of friends and she was very fond of him and at times the future seemed very bleak without someone to care for her, even though she realised with absolute clarity that it would be much more a case of caring for Daniel. He was dependent on his family for so much, the everyday conveniences of living. If she married him, he would simply transfer the burden of that dependence to her shoulders and she did not deceive herself that it would not be a burden to carry for the rest of her life.

It would delight her aunt, she knew. For she dearly loved Daniel and naturally fretted about his future. Marriage to someone as concerned and as capable as Ruth would solve every problem in her view—and, like any mother, she would not hesitate to sacrifice Ruth's happiness to secure the comfort, convenience and well-being of her only son.

A trained nurse who was also a close friend because of the family connection must seem the ideal wife for a man in Daniel's position. She only had to accept that she would always be nurse, companion and substitute mother and never truly a wife.

Ruth had always felt that she would never love again. Her heart had been too bruised, too shocked, by a man who had not loved or needed her. So it had not seemed so impossible or so wrong that she should marry Daniel who did care for her and did need her and would not expect her to love him because he knew all about Neil and those dreadful weeks of heartbreak.

But last night, out of the blue, she had discovered an unsuspected sensuality in her nature. She had felt a fierce physical desire for a man who had not triggered it with the least touch or word or glance. She had been shocked, a little ashamed of wanting a man who did not want her, and thankful that the moment had passed without betrayal. Oliver had not suspected that sudden need. She had moved away from him, sat in a chair as far as possible from him in that small room and maintained the cool neutrality that had always typified their relationship. Only at the moment of leaving, her hand clasped in his strong fingers, had she weakened and yielded to that ridiculous impulse to touch her lips to his cheek. Had she hoped he might stay, sweep her into his arms and satisfy that almost frightening longing for a fulfilment she had never known?

Now she wondered if she could marry Daniel, if he asked her, knowing that the sexual relationship was impossible for him and that her natural instincts, newly awakened by another man's physical magnetism, would always be frustrated. Was it fair to Daniel—or to herself?

But if she refused him, what did the future hold, she wondered bleakly. For there would never be another Neil. And if some kind of chemistry had made her physically aware of Oliver, she knew enough about him to realise that he would offer nothing but a brief and destructive affair. She would be the loser like all the women before her.

So was she to spend her entire life at Hartlake, never knowing the ecstasy and fulfilment to be found in a man's arms? Or should she marry Daniel—and suffer the same fate?

Sylvia Seaton came out to the terrace to join them with a tray of tea. To Ruth's relief, there was no further talk of personalities. She understood that Daniel was jealous and was glad that he did not know how her body responded to Oliver Manning, even if her heart was untouched by the fatal charm of this man.

It was a very pleasant afternoon. Ruth enjoyed the relaxation, the warm sunshine, the congenial company.

70

It was very much her second home. Her parents were divorced and her mother lived in the Cotswolds. Her father had remarried and lived and worked in Germany. So Ruth had come to regard the Seatons as much more her family these days.

Daniel was in great spirits and he had always been able to make her laugh. His lively sense of humour matched her own—one of the things that sometimes tempted her to spend the rest of her life with him. He was very interested in her work, too, and she found much to tell him about Hartlake and the patients—and remembered too late that she had intended to talk to Oliver about Miss Mallow.

In the early evening, some of Daniel's friends dropped in for a cool beer and a chat. The girls had slipped out of his life, one by one. The men remained loyal to a mate who never grumbled about his rotten luck, always made them welcome and took a healthy interest in their male pursuits. They were young and exuberant and they flirted a little with Ruth under Daniel's amused but watchful eyes.

On the still evening air, the sound of the telephone carried clearly out to the terrace. Sylvia Seaton reluctantly stirred in her comfortable chair. "Now I wonder who that can be . . ."

"I'll answer it, shall I?" Ruth smiled at her aunt and stood up.

"It's probably your uncle to say that he's going to be late for dinner," she said dryly. Donald Seaton was a haulage contractor and his hours were always erratic. Throughout the years, he had seen little of his wife and son and perhaps that was one of the reasons why her aunt was so devoted to Daniel, Ruth thought, going into

71

the cool house to answer the shrill summons.

It was Oliver. Ruth did not immediately recognise the voice that spoke her name so confidently—and then she was staggered. For how had he known the number?

"Looked it up in the directory," he said easily. "Thought you might still be there, Ruth. Do you want a lift home? I can call for you in half an hour if that's convenient."

"You're still in Woodford?" she said, surprised.

"A little further out, actually. I looked up some friends."

She had not been looking forward to the journey and it did not seem as though her uncle was going to be home in time to drive her as he sometimes did. "Well, I'd love it," she said frankly. "If you're quite sure . . ."

"My pleasure," he said warmly.

Ruth heard the little click as he replaced the receiver. He had sounded very casual, very matter of fact, as though it was the most natural thing in the world that he should ring her up out of the blue and propose to take her home. But it was not like him to show her so much consideration, she thought, baffled. Why was he being so kind, so thoughtful?

She went to explain to Daniel and her aunt and tried not to see the little frown in those very blue eyes or notice the hint of disapproval in her aunt's manner. She was already regarded by Sylvia Seaton as her son's future wife and any other man in her life was seen as a threat to his happiness, Ruth realised with a little jolt of apprehension. She had come very near to slipping into the rôle without a word of protest and she could not blame Daniel or his mother.

Later, sliding into the seat beside Oliver, she knew

that her heart fluttered as she met the dark, smiling eyes. She ought to have been firm about refusing his offer. It was probably nothing more than friendliness on his part but her response to him was too swift, too alarming—and much too physical to be trusted.

"This is very nice of you," she said lightly, as coolly as she could. "But you are spoiling me, you know."

"I shouldn't think that happens often enough," Oliver returned promptly.

She turned to send a last wave to her aunt, watching from the gate. Daniel had cried off from meeting Oliver, disappearing in the direction of the bathroom as the car was heard to draw up outside the house.

Oliver glanced briefly at the small, suddenly animated face, warmed by the kiss of the sun, and wondered why he felt so drawn to her that he had cancelled a dinner engagement for the doubtful pleasure of driving all the way to Woodford in order to take her home with only her gratitude for reward. He did not doubt that she was pleased and grateful. She was also puzzled by his attentions, he thought dryly. Well, it puzzled him, too.

Ruth settled herself comfortably in the seat beside him. "A girl could get used to this kind of luxury. It's a beautiful car, Oliver. But doesn't it cost a fortune to run?"

He laughed. "Very nearly! But it seems that a consultant is expected to drive a Rolls to keep up his image. And it suits me, don't you think?"

Ruth considered him, head on one side, eyes bright with merriment. "I think a little more grey and a lot more paunch, actually. Ten years from now, perhaps." She added tentatively; "You'll be married by then, of course—and your wife won't approve of other women travelling in your car."

"I expect you're right," he said easily. "Hospital governors do like their consultants to be married . . . the aura of respectability, I suppose."

His words reminded her of the lovely Hilary Longhurst who was so glamorous and sophisticated and expensive—just like his gleaming Rolls Royce. Obviously the perfect wife for a successful consultant, and just the kind of girl to appeal to a man like Oliver. Ruth wondered if she had really thought for one foolish moment that he found her attractive when she was so plain and dull and ordinary in comparison with most of the girls in his life, let alone Hilary Longhurst!

She said brightly: "Won't you find it very boring to be respectable, Oliver? You aren't the type to settle for one woman." Her teasing tone traded on the years they had known each other, robbed the words of any personal interest in his future plans.

"That depends on the woman," he told her, smiling. "But I don't mean to rush into marriage just to please the Board of Governors. Hartlake would be strewn with bruised and bleeding hearts . . . and the juniors need someone like me to dream about while they are taking temps and issuing bedpans and being scolded by hard-hearted Sisters."

Ruth laughed at him gently. "You are so conceited!" she declared, almost in earnest. For he had never been unconscious of his good looks or his charm, she thought dryly. He had used them to his advantage too many times. It was annoying to find that she was not as immune to them as she had always believed. She had often deplored the weakness of the girls who were ready to fall

74

into his arms at one smile and one meaningful glance from those dark eyes—yet she was dangerously close to doing the same thing!

"But lovely with it." His eyes twinkling, he touched the back of his long fingers to her soft cheek in a careless caress . . . a gesture of friendliness, of shared amusement.

Nothing more, of course—but a little tremor rippled through her body at his touch and her heart seemed to turn over. She was alarmed, a little annoyed. For surely she was not going to be so silly as to like him too much!

It was not a question of loving, of course. Nothing so highflown, she thought dryly. He was very *physical* . . . the type she had never liked or trusted in the past. His very magnetism spoke of the thrill of the chase and the delights of the conquest for a man like Oliver Manning. She knew all about the long list of his women—and wished he did not tug so fiercely at her senses.

She had never quite understood the force of physical attraction—or felt it until now. She had seen it at work and knew it could bring a great deal of unhappiness to the men who made fools of themselves and the women who were ready to sacrifice everything for its sake.

She had loved Neil and looked forward to being his wife but sex had played a very minor part in their relationship. Very young and rather naïve, she had not then realised that her coolness was probably a major factor in his retreat from marriage at almost the last moment. Men attached importance to that kind of thing, she had discovered, wondering. Yet Neil had not seemed impatient or particularly ardent. Too inexperienced for relief or disappointment, she had not given his attitude very much thought.

Now, suddenly, she found that a man's touch could make her tremble, melt inside, long for the embrace that would transport her to the world of sexual delight to which she was still a stranger. A man she scarcely knew and was only just learning to like had the power to arouse a pulse-quickening excitement that alarmed her and she knew she should draw back from a dangerous threshold. For surely loving ought to be the only key to that particular heaven . . .

As the car pulled up outside the house, she turned to him with reserve in her manner. "Thank you so much for bringing me home. I am grateful."

The brush-off, Oliver told himself ruefully, wondering how he had offended. He had thought that they were getting on very well. He was not so much disappointed as dismayed that she did not like him better, trust him more. It was going to be more difficult than he had dreamed to break through that cool reserve, that obvious indifference. Perhaps he just could not compete with Cousin Daniel.

"You do know that I had an ulterior motive, of course," he said softly, a little devil dancing in his dark eyes. She looked at him, doubtfully, and stiffened. His heart melted at that vulnerable and touching innocence. It was a shame to tease her. "No one makes coffee quite the way you do."

She relaxed, as he had intended. She said, smiling; "I don't believe that for a moment! But I can take a hint, I hope. Won't you come in for a quick cup of coffee before you go on your way?"

Amused, he said lightly: "I can take a hint, too, you know."

Meeting the kindly laughter in his eyes, Ruth was

covered in confusion. Had she been too obvious in her anxiety to keep him at a safe distance? How silly when he probably had no real desire to come any closer! She was just making a fool of herself like the most junior of first-year student nurses who supposed that any man who looked at her twice must have evil designs on her virtue!

CHAPTER SIX

When Ruth came out of the kitchen after switching on the electric kettle, she found Oliver stretched full length on the sofa, hands behind his head, very much at ease. He smiled at her, an oddly youthful smile that caught at her heart.

"I like it here," he announced with the air of one bestowing the accolade. "It's a nice little flat, Ruth."

She raised an eyebrow. "You weren't very complimentary about it last night, I remember."

"Well, I've changed my mind. This place has atmosphere."

"That's the damp patches," she said in her no-nonsense voice.

Oliver laughed. "Perhaps. But it's a home, you know, Ruth . . . friendly, welcoming, warm. My flat is the usual bachelor pad . . . purely functional. It lacks the feminine touch."

"I should have thought there'd been enough women in your flat to give it a feminine touch," she said lightly, teasing him, careful to keep even the slightest dislike of those other women from her voice.

He shrugged. "Good-time girls," he drawled. "Nothing like you, Ruth . . ." No sense in denying something that she knew as well as he did. There had been a lot of women in his life. Beautiful, amusing, sophisticated . . . knowing all the answers, taking much and giving little. A man grew older and wiser and began to want more from a woman than the fleeting gratification of a sexual need.

"So I should imagine," she said, a trifle dryly, thinking of the kind of girl who usually attracted Oliver Manning—the typical honeypot that captivated all the men. Nothing like herself, indeed, she thought with a touch of bitterness and wondered why he was bothering to spend even a little time in her company when she could not compare with the women he had known.

Oliver followed her into the kitchen. "Need any help?"

He seemed so big, so masculine, so dominant in that tiny space where there was scarcely room for one person to turn round. Ruth found him much too close for comfort and her heart began to pound.

"I don't think there's anything you can do," she said brightly. She busied herself with the coffee jar, very aware of him and wondering if he knew it. A man with his experience must know a great deal about women and be very sure of his effect on them, she thought.

Oliver wandered out. With a new interest in everything that affected Ruth, he looked about the small but comfortable living room. Her books, her records, her taste in pictures were little details of her life that he suddenly needed to know.

A photograph, framed and standing on a corner unit, caught his eye for the first time. He walked across to study it. It was a snapshot of a muscular young man: laughing, handsome, very much a man, the zest for living and loving coming through clearly for all the neutrality of the black and white print.

The fact that she valued the photograph enough to frame it and keep it in a prominent position gave him pause. Was it possible that there was more than ordinary family affection and feminine compassion behind those regular visits to Cousin Daniel? Had she transferred all the intensity of her youthful devotion from one familiar figure to another?

Ruth came in with the coffee. He turned, indicated the photograph. "Your cousin?"

"Yes, that's Daniel. That was taken just a few weeks before the car crash. You can see what a tragedy it was!"

"Good-looking chap," Oliver commented.

"Yes, isn't he?" Her tone was eager, pleased. "It's the beard, I think. It gives him such a dashing, romantic air." She blushed a little as his smile deepened. "Well, it *does*!" she insisted, slightly on the defensive.

Oliver sat down beside her on the sofa. "You are very fond of him, aren't you?" His tone was carefully casual.

"I admire him so much," she said warmly. "He's adapted amazingly well to a totally different way of life. It takes courage but he has plenty of that. Oh yes, I'm very fond of Daniel. We're great friends."

Oliver reached for his coffee. "Just friends?" She hesitated and the little silence alarmed him, sent him blundering into speech like any callow youth. "Mean to marry him, do you?" He looked at her with a little smile flickering in his dark eyes.

Ruth's chin tilted. His expression seemed to be mocking as though he doubted that any man would want to marry her. Did he think they were all like Neil, or himself?

"I might," she said, proud.

He was suddenly very sure that she was not in love

80

with the man. His spirits rose. No doubt Cousin Daniel wanted her. A man matured by suffering rather than years would certainly recognise the pure gold of Ruth's warm and generous nature and she might be tempted by his obvious need of her.

Oliver had seen her dedication to nursing, her devotion to the patients in her care. She responded instinctively to their need of her without a thought for herself no matter how weary or anxious or unhappy she might be. She was an excellent nurse. She would be a wonderful wife for any man that persuaded her into marriage and it would not be so difficult if she could be convinced that she was needed. He fancied that might mean more to Ruth than being loved. She was wary of love, having found that it was not always true or lasting.

He said lightly: "Why not? You ought to marry, have children. A good nurse always makes a good wife and mother, I've observed. Cousin Daniel would be a fortunate man if you married him."

Instantly Ruth resented his readiness to push her into marriage with a man he did not even know—and she felt that it was typically male arrogance that he should be more concerned with Daniel's good than her own. And his words reminded her forcibly that such a marriage would be far from satisfactory. She had all a woman's normal, healthy instincts but she would not be truly a wife and she would never be mother to Daniel's children. It was not surprising that she was so reluctant to encourage his anxious mother to plan or the hopeful Daniel to propose a marriage between them.

"I haven't made up my mind yet," she said airily, letting him suppose that she had been asked. It was a little prop for her pride. "I've worked hard for my ward,

Oliver. I don't think I want to give it all up just yet . . . and looking after Daniel would be a full-time job, of course."

It seemed to Oliver that there was a very real danger that she would marry her cousin. The man she had once loved had hurt her badly. Instinctively she turned towards the familiar, the trusted. The physical resemblance between Neil Plummer and Cousin Daniel, the blond beard excepted, had not escaped him even if Ruth might be unaware of it. He wondered how he could keep her from doing anything so foolish as to marry a very poor substitute for her lost love.

His liking and admiration and respect for her had grown steadily and suddenly he was very near to loving her. But she did not trust him, he thought ruefully. She had not known him well enough for long enough—and he had that well-earned reputation as a Casanova to overcome! However, he hoped that she was beginning to like him. It was a foundation on which to build if only she would give him the time and the opportunity.

"You would be very much missed if you left Hartlake," he told her quietly, taking refuge in the impersonal.

Professionally, she thought, a little bleakly. If he never saw her again, she would be swiftly forgotten by him. "Oh, I meant to ask you about Miss Mallow," she suddenly remembered. "You were with her when she died, weren't you?"

"She went happily to meet her Maker, I think. She told me that she'd enjoyed this life but was quite ready to begin a new one." He spoke lightly but very tenderly of the old lady.

Ruth put her hand on his arm, a little shyly. "She was

82

eighty-four, Oliver," she reminded him gently, sure that it had been a blow for him to lose this particular patient.

"Yes, I know." He turned his head to look at her. "She thanked me . . . did you know? That was a new experience. Grateful patients due for discharge have been known to utter the odd word of thanks but it's never happened with someone who might have had a few more months or even years if I hadn't interfered."

Ruth heard the faint bitterness. "You did what you had to do," she said firmly. "And perhaps you spared her months of pain. Do look at it that way." She might have been comforting a grieving relative.

He said wryly: "I am seldom so involved—I try not to be. In my position, one feels a little like God at times with the power of life or death in one's hands. I can't allow personal feelings to affect a decision. You're absolutely right, Ruth. I had to operate or allow her to suffer—and that isn't a choice for a surgeon who is dedicated to eradicating disease, is it?"

"I'm so glad that you were with her. She trusted you," she said quietly.

"Yes. Opportune, wasn't it? No one should have to die alone," he returned carelessly.

Ruth was not deceived by the casual tone. Like herself, like any member of their profession, he had seen much of death. But he could still be moved—and she warmed to him.

"Did you have a premonition?" she asked, curious.

He shrugged, smiled. "Nothing so fanciful. I just wanted to look in on her before going to bed and chose the right moment to do so." He changed the subject. "By the way, we were talking of Levitovski last night. I believe you said that you'd like to hear his recital at the

Festival Hall. Well, I managed to get seats if you'd like to go with me.''

She turned a surprised and delighted face to him, eager, animated, suddenly a girl. "But they are like gold-dust, Oliver! I tried every agent in London! How on earth did you get tickets?''

He felt that odd little contraction of his heart. The pleasure in her small face gave it a very special beauty in his eyes. "Oh, I have influence," he said lightly. He did not explain that he had spent much of the afternoon after leaving her in Woodford in tracking down a friend who could help and who owed him a favour. "Friends in high places . . .''

"But that's wonderful!''

He smiled into the sparkling green eyes. "I'm glad you are pleased.''

Ruth was thrilled by the promised delight of the music, of hearing the internationally famous pianist in person. But she was much more pleased by his unexpected kindness, by the fact that he had noted a wish expressed in casual conversation and gone out of his way to fulfil it.

"I don't know what to say, how to thank you," she said, a little unsteadily. "You must have gone to a lot of trouble.''

"No trouble at all," he told her lightly. "And to know that you are pleased is all the thanks I need.''

He put an arm about her shoulders and felt the swift tensing of her body, heard the sharp intake of her breath. She was so slight, so seemingly fragile in his embrace, that he was engulfed by a wave of protective tenderness, unlike anything he had ever known. He bent his dark head to kiss her, very fleetingly, meaning to reassure her and believing that the light and merely friendly touch of his lips must convince her that while he wanted her, he could wait until she knew him better, liked him more.

Ruth was very still, startled by his embrace, terrified that the leaping excitement within her would betray itself. What did he want of her? she wondered, her heart cavorting in her breast. That they should be friends—or lovers? Had she caught his fickle interest without even trying? She ought not to be flattered by the attentions of a womaniser with a long string of conquests to his credit. She thought of his rumoured affair with Hilary Longhurst that would possibly lead to marriage—and knew that if he did want her, it was only for amusement.

But if she rejected him, she would lose even the friendship which suddenly meant a lot to her. He was proud, as sensitive as any man. He could be very cold, very distant. She had seen his manner change from warmth to ice overnight when an affair ended or a friend offended. Unexpectedly, she was basking in the warmth of his interest and attention—and she was enjoying it, she admitted frankly. She would be oddly chilled by a return to his former polite, careless indifference.

Her treacherous body responded to him with alarming urgency. She was painfully aware of the weight of his arm on her slight shoulders. Her heart was thudding against her ribs, her mouth was dry, her body clamouring to know more of the secret world hinted at in his touch, his nearness, the smiling warmth in his dark eyes.

Her lips parted suddenly, quivered beneath his own. Oliver's heart quickened and so did desire. She sought his hand and took it to her breast, so naturally, so trustingly, that he was shaken. It was a sweet gesture of surrender that he had not expected from someone as shy and modest as Ruth. It touched him to the depths of his being.

They kissed and she clung to him, fingers entwined in the dark curls at the nape of his neck, her slight body trembling with eagerness. Oliver's hands shook as he unbuttoned her shirt and slipped it from her shoulders, unclipped the bra and freed the beautiful breasts from confinement. He kissed her more urgently, caressed her into a feverish pitch of wanting.

Suddenly, with one swift movement, he rose and swept her up into his arms and carried her through to the bedroom. He laid her on the bed and she smiled at him shakily. He looked down at her, hesitating. Not since his salad days at university had he been so fierce with desire, so fearful of disappointment, so unsure of himself. "Sure, Ruth . . .?"

She nodded, held out her arms to him. He bent down to kiss her. With very gentle hands, he undressed her between kisses . . . and it took all his considerable experience, all his strength of mind, to control the rising tide of his own excitement so that he should not disappoint her.

He stripped out of his own clothes and she opened her arms to receive him as a lover, shy but eager to *know*, to fulfil her womanhood.

Suddenly, with his body hard against her own, she panicked. "No . . . oh no!" she said, burying her face in the hollows of his neck.

"Yes, oh yes," Oliver said gently but very firmly. He put a hand beneath her chin and tilted her face to kiss her. "Trust me," he murmured against her lips and her arms tightened about him, drew him close . . .

Oliver had made love to more women than he could remember and few of them had meant very much to him. But making love to Ruth was a totally new and very wonderful experience.

He had suspected that she was a virgin. He had never imagined that she could be so warm, so tender, so generous or so joyful in her response to his expertise as a lover. He had not expected to be swept along with her ecstasy to heights that he had never known.

He had thought her shy, a little cold, a most unlikely conquest. He found that she was entirely at ease with him, swiftly kindled to desire by his touch . . . and she had conquered him utterly with that simple and moving gesture of surrender. He had never known anyone quite like her, he thought. She was very sweet, wholly enchanting—and he knew that she did not love him at all.

That was the most surprising part of it, he decided ruefully. For he would have sworn that Ruth was the kind of girl who needed to be in love—or needed to *believe* herself in love—before she would go to bed with any man. He gave heartfelt thanks that destiny or whatever had decreed that he should be the man to awaken her dormant sexuality so abruptly.

Spent but utterly content, he lay beside her in the narrow bed, her head cradled on his shoulder, the lovely hair released from its pins and tumbling about her small face, the naked shoulders, the beautiful breasts. She looked very lovely to his eyes and he marvelled that he had ever supposed her to be plain or unattractive or of little interest to him. Life, and love, could play some odd tricks.

His arm tightened about her and he brushed her forehead with his lips. For the first time in his life, he longed to speak of loving, of needing, even of marrying, as he held her in the golden glow that was the aftermath of passion. He knew that he loved her very much, as he had never expected to love any woman. He knew, too, that this was not the moment to say so. She would not believe him.

Ruth lay against him, trembling still, and wondering. The tumult of wave upon wave of desire and the incredible magic of that mutual and ecstatic triumph had taught her the sheer potency of the sexual act between a man and a woman. She had known the power and the glory, she thought tremulously. His, the power with that lean, hard body to transport her to a new and wonderful world. Hers, the glory of giving for his delight.

At the same time, it was a little frightening to realise that she could never go back to being a virgin—and that she and Oliver must always be linked by that brief bond of intimacy although they might and probably would go their separate ways in life. For a brief period of ecstasy, they had been as one and it was unforgettable, unalterable.

Ruth had no regrets. She had wanted desperately to *know* . . . and now she knew. If she never found again that secret world of delight, she had been there once and knew it to be glorious beyond all description. But she understood now why Puritans insisted that mutual loving should be the only key to that heaven. For the experience was too meaningful for casual coupling between strangers.

She felt his lips at her temple, light, lazily caressing. *Darling,* he had said in that fantastic, never to be forgotten moment when passion had reached its climactic peak . . . *darling*.

Just a word, she thought. She had been too caught up in the magic to speak at all. She could only cling to him. Just a word. But she would always hear the infinite tenderness in his voice when she was alone and quiet and remembering. It was a memory to cherish without even knowing why.

Suddenly she shivered.

"Ruth, you're cold!" he said swiftly, gathering her close.

"No . . ." Ruth pulled away from him, sat up. She felt the stirrings of fear deep within her. She had loved once and been so badly hurt that she carried the scars still on her heart and her pride. She did not mean to love again. She would not love this man who did not know the meaning of the word and had been to bed with so many women that it tore her to pieces to think about it. She rejected a mental picture of another woman in that magical embrace, knowing such delight, hearing him say 'darling' in just that way when pleasure was at its peak.

Oliver raised himself on an elbow, kissed her bare shoulder. He looked at that small, set face and his heart contracted. "What is it?"

"Shouldn't you go home, Oliver?" Her tone was cool, dismissive.

He rolled over to look at his watch. "It isn't so late," he discovered. He chuckled softly. "Respectable people aren't even in bed yet."

She flinched. "I want you to go."

Reaction, he thought in swift understanding. It hit different women in different ways. But the quiet, implacable tone hurt him. The warm and very precious intimacy between them was abruptly shattered by an unmistakable note of rejection.

"Perhaps it would be wise," he agreed, a little reluctantly, choosing to misunderstand her concern. "Next time I must park my car in a less conspicuous place. We don't really want the world to know that we are lovers, do we?" He smiled, moved to kiss her on the words.

Ruth averted her face. "We aren't lovers and there won't be a next time, Oliver." She did not care what he thought of her, she told herself defiantly. It was too dangerous to continue with this new and demanding relationship.

She was overwrought, Oliver told himself, refusing to believe that she meant what she said. But she was very calm, very composed and he was alarmed, knowing how important she had become to him, how much he needed her in his life.

"This isn't like you, Ruth," he said gently, putting an arm about her, brushing the soft sweep of her hair from her face.

She moved from him suddenly, leaving the bed, reaching for something, anything, to cover her nudity. "How can you say what is like me or what isn't? We scarcely know each other," she said brusquely.

"I know every inch of you," he told her, his dark eyes suddenly brimming with merriment. She blushed and he was moved by her youth, that hint of shyness. He reached towards her, holding out his hand, smiling with tender warmth. "Come back to bed," he coaxed. "To hell with the gossips. I want to spend the night with you, sleep with you, wake up with you in my arms and make love to you again. I want you, Ruth," he added more urgently as desire again stirred abruptly. He touched her breast in the light caress of the lover, felt her body quiver. "It's a wonderful way to get to know each other," he said softly.

He was very persuasive.

Ruth shook her head, fighting temptation. "I want you to go," she said again, in that hard little voice.

Hurt, baffled, Oliver was also very angry. Proud, he had never beseeched any woman in his life to love him, need him . . . never needed to, damn it! He swung from the bed and reached for his clothes without another word. He went into the tiny bathroom.

When he returned, dressed, smoothing his dark hair with his hands, Ruth was stripping the sheets from the bed. She had wrapped a thin silk robe tightly about her slender body.

She looked at him with guarded eyes. "I'm going to Manchester tomorrow for a few days," he said carefully. "May I see you when I get back?" He spoke lightly as though it did not matter more than anything else in the world.

"I don't want to see you again, Oliver." Her voice was low but determined.

He raised an eyebrow. "There has to be a reason."

"There is. I'm going to marry Daniel. I've made up my mind," she said, surprising herself. But it was the first thing that came into her head and she used it, knowing that she had no easily explained reason for wanting nothing more to do with Oliver Manning.

He did not believe her. He was suddenly filled with love, with tender understanding. He smiled at her gently. "Do you have to know me twenty years before you'll begin to trust me," he said, a little ruefully.

Colour surged into her small face. "It isn't a question of trust . . ."

"Yes, it is, Ruth. You're afraid I shall run away just as Neil did if you allow yourself to care for me," he said quietly. "I imagine you've felt like that about every man for the last three years. But you mustn't cling to Cousin Daniel just because he can't run away, you know." He was deliberately blunt, trying to shock her into realising the danger in that direction.

She was suddenly furious. "That's horrible!" she said fiercely.

"It could be," Oliver agreed dryly.

CHAPTER SEVEN

Always so cheerful, so placid and unruffled even in emergency, Ruth found that she was snapping at her young nurses and feeling rushed off her feet during those few days when Oliver was in Manchester. It was not that she missed him or wanted to see him again, she told herself firmly, even while she wondered if she had offended beyond forgiveness when she insisted on him leaving her or if he would get in touch with her as soon as he returned to London.

Things reached their peak on the day that he was due to return. Nothing went right on the ward. Mrs Junkin pulled out her drainage tube. Mrs Marshall's drip refused to work properly and had to be set up again by an overworked houseman. Mrs Wainwright began to haemorrhage and had to be rushed back to Theatres. The newest of her first-years broke a thermometer, stepped back in dismay and sent a dressings-trolley crashing to the floor. She burst into tears and rushed down the ward to collide with Oliver Manning as he entered through the swing doors.

Ruth's heart lurched, making her feel quite sick. The crash of the trolley had brought her from her office to investigate and she was not prepared for the sight of Oliver, steadying Nurse Sims with a swift hand, his warm smile and pleasant voice doing much to distract the girl's mind from all the disaster in her wake. Blushing and confused, the junior escaped into the sluice to pull herself together and Oliver, meeting Ruth's gaze, began to walk towards her.

She wished that *she* could snatch a few moments of privacy in which to pull herself together. For her heart had reacted with ridiculous delight to his dark good looks, his vibrant masculinity. It was not one of his days to be at Hartlake in any capacity. Perhaps she had hoped that he might telephone but she had not expected or wished to see him walk into the ward.

She beckoned to Nurse Trevor. "Clear up that mess immediately, please, Nurse. And tell Nurse Sims to report to me in ten minutes in a clean apron and with her cap straight and her face washed!"

"Yes, Sister." The girl hastened away.

She really was a Sister Booth in the making, Ruth told herself bleakly, and turned to greet Oliver with the coolest of smiles.

During the few days of his absence, she had thought and thought and come to the same conclusion. It would be madness to go on seeing him, to risk falling in love with him. She had witnessed too much of the heartache he had caused. She had seen too many girls suffering all the misery of caring for a man who seemed incapable of caring at all. He was flirtatious and fickle and quite without heart—not to be trusted!

But she refused to regret that one precious hour she had spent in his arms. A girl had to store up a few lovely memories against a bleak old age, she told herself, a little wry. But the experience must never be repeated. Her heart was her own again after a long and aching sadness. She meant to hold on to it!

94

"Good afternoon, Mr Manning." She was briskly professional, the capable ward sister from head to toe, from frilled and starched cap to sensible black shoes.

"Good afternoon, Sister." He was just as formal but his eyes twinkled, mischievously reminding her that she had not been so stiff and starchy at their last encounter. "Can you spare me a few moments? I won't keep you long."

He knew that it was impossible for her to refuse, she thought crossly. He was taking an unfair advantage. "Certainly. Shall we go into my office?" She knew that he had come to discuss personal rather than professional matters and it surprised her that he was so persistent when there were so many other girls, prettier and more willing to please him. She sat down at her desk, turning it into a barrier. "Well . . .?"

Tone and manner were far from encouraging. Oliver perched on the edge of the desk and smiled at her with a certain tenderness in his dark eyes that no other woman had ever seen.

"I know you're busy. I know I'm breaking all the rules by being here—and you're frowning at me just as Sister Booth always did. She didn't approve of me any more than you do. But I wanted to see you, Ruth," he told her with truth. Wanting had been an insistent ache during those days in Manchester, centred as much in the region of his heart as in his loins, proof if he had needed it that he was truly in love at last. "I've missed you . . ."

She smiled coolly, not believing him. He was a sensual man, far too attractive for his own good. No doubt there had been a girl in Manchester. For a man like Oliver, there would always be a girl, she told herself harshly, so perhaps it was just as well that he had no wife to make miserable. Foolishly, it hurt her to think of him in another woman's embrace—and she had no right to his loyalty.

"How was Manchester?" she asked lightly.

"Irksome. I wanted to be in London." He noticed that her slender fingers were fretting the corner of the blotter on her desk. That restlessness betrayed her, he thought gently, remembering how much he had always admired her quality of stillness. He was disturbing her for all that air of composure. His heart lifted.

He covered her hand with his own. Her fingers were stilled, tense. She would not look at him. He curled his fingers about hers, lifted her hand towards his lips. She resisted. He persisted and pressed a light kiss into the palm of her hand.

"For heaven's sake, Oliver . . ." Impatient, sure that they were observed through the plate glass window that overlooked the ward, she snatched her hand away. His every move was of absurd interest to her impressionable nurses, she thought, annoyed with him. "Do give a thought to my position!"

"If I didn't, you'd be in my arms," he told her bluntly.

She looked at him then, coldly. "You're much too sure of yourself."

"I'd like to be sure of you," he said promptly.

She half-rose from the desk. "Look, I just haven't the time for this kind of thing . . ."

"Now—or never?" He smiled but he was tense, waiting for her reply.

She hesitated. This was the moment to be firm, to end it all. "I told you, Oliver. I'm going to marry Daniel," she said, a little desperately.

He relaxed and now his engaging smile crinkled the

dark eyes. "That doesn't mean that we can't be friends."

She met his eyes squarely. "I won't be your lover, Oliver," she said, meaning it. "I'm not a cheat and I'm not promiscuous."

He put a hand beneath her chin and he was no longer smiling but very, very serious. "I like your company, Ruth. Anything more is a bonus as far as I'm concerned."

Any woman would have been flattered by the quiet words and their seeming sincerity. Ruth was no exception. But her eyes still held a little doubt. "If I do go out with you again one evening, you truly won't try to make love to me?"

That little imp of mischief lurked in his smiling eyes. "If I wasn't a gentleman, I might be tempted to remind you that I didn't make the first move," he said softly— and watched with tender delight as the soft blush stole into her cheeks.

He loved her very much. And, like any man in love, he wanted her with fierce, sexual urgency. He knew how swiftly responsive and excitingly eager that lovely body could be in his embrace. He knew that no other woman had ever given him such delight, such satisfaction. It would probably be the nearest thing to purgatory to be with her and have to keep a tight rein on the passion she stirred in him. But if that was the way she wanted it, then he was prepared to accept her terms until she learned to trust him and, perhaps, to love him. Anything must be better than never seeing her outside the coldly impersonal bricks and mortar of a hospital!

Taking pity on that shy embarrassment that was such a marked contrast to her uninhibited response to his lovemaking, Oliver produced his wallet and opened it, drawing out the tickets for the Levitovski recital at the Festival Hall. "If you didn't show any signs of relenting, I meant to wave these under your nose," he said lightly. "It's tonight, you know. That's why I had to see you this afternoon. You will come, won't you?"

Ruth saw that the tickets were for the very best seats. A faint anticipatory excitement stirred in her breast. "Oh, dear," she said helplessly. "I don't think I've the strength of mind to refuse." And she smiled at him suddenly, enchantingly youthful.

Oliver laughed and moved towards the door. "We all have our little weaknesses." He paused and looked at her with a rueful expression in his dark eyes. "It seems that you are one of mine, Sister Challis."

She remained at her desk after the door had closed on him, very still. She had meant to be so firm, so resolute. In the face of that warm and endearing charm, she was lost. It seemed that when it came to admitting weaknesses, Oliver Manning was the most dangerous of hers, she thought wryly.

She had dreaded the inevitable first meeting. She had expected to be shy and ill at ease, much too conscious of all that had passed between them on that unforgettable night. But, except for that gentle and perfectly acceptable teasing, there had been nothing at all to embarrass her in his manner. There had been much to confound and bewilder her, however. For she could not think why he was so attentive, so persistent, so set on being her friend. People said that a man lost interest as soon as he had taken what he wanted from a woman. Well, Oliver had not seemed to want her at all until, as he had pointed out, she had made the first move—and then he had obviously not lost interest. And not only that, he had surprisingly agreed to her demand for a platonic relationship in the future!

Ruth decided it was very heart-warming to be liked for herself, to be sought after for reasons other than sexual, to know that he enjoyed her company for its own sake and to feel that he really could be content with simple friendship in these permissive times.

Suddenly she realised that she had gained nothing—and here she was complimenting herself on having managed things to her satisfaction! She had been determined to have nothing more to do with him except as her work demanded and yet she was committed to going to a piano recital with him that very evening! If she yielded so easily to the first temptation that came along, how could she hope to keep him sufficiently at a distance to avoid loving him?

Her fearful heart told her that it would be very foolish to encourage him any further. Her level head reminded her crisply that she could not be more encouraging than she had already been. It was rather too late to declare that she did not like or trust him. She liked him too much, in truth. She had leaped into bed with him and no one could be more trusting than that, she thought wryly.

"Come . . ." she called absently to a timid knock on the door.

Nurse Sims hesitated, desperately hoping that her wretched cap wasn't slowly sliding over one ear as usual. Her plump cheeks were bright red from the cold water and the briskly-applied flannel. Her blue eyes were wide and apprehensive. She went in, heart pounding at thought of the scold in store for her. She had only been a few days on Paterson but she had already discovered that Sister Challis had a sharp tongue which belied the

99

sweetness of her smile.

"What is it, Nurse?" Ruth regarded her new junior with indulgent eyes. She was very young and eager to please and a natural clumsiness was enhanced by nervousness. But she was a friendly child who seemed to know instinctively when a patient was uncomfortable or anxious which was a very big mark in her favour. When she had settled down and acquired a little confidence, she would probably be an asset on the ward. At the moment, she was a walking disaster area.

Phyllida Sims stared. "Didn't you want to see me, Sister? Nurse Trevor told me to report to you."

Ruth remembered—and observed that the girl had failed to change her apron as she had certainly been told to do. Perhaps she had been too busy with that unequal struggle between her cap and the thick mop of curls to remember her apron.

"Yes, of course. You've been wreaking havoc again, Nurse Sims," she said gently. Her smile was very warm.

Phyllida's heart quietened. Sister was in a surprisingly good humour in contrast to her mood earlier in the day. Perhaps Mr Manning's visit to the ward had brought that sparkle to her eyes and that faint colour to her face and that new tolerance to her tone. Still, he was far too attractive to throw himself away on the plain, unexciting Sister Challis.

"Yes, Sister. I'm sorry, Sister," she said in automatic response.

"And I'm sure that Sister Tutor impressed on you that a nurse never runs except in case of fire or haemorrhage?"

"Yes, Sister."

"But you were running when I saw you, Nurse Sims

100

". . . the whole length of the ward!"

"I'm sorry, Sister."

"Goodness knows what Mr Manning thought of my nurses!"

A smile leaped to Phyllida's lips. "He asked if it was a fire and I said that was yesterday when Mrs Lindley was smoking in bed and then he said perhaps haemorrhage and I said that was this morning with Mrs Wainwright and he laughed and said that he'd obviously missed all the excitement and . . ."

"That will do, Nurse." Checking the flow in midstream, Ruth thought it scarcely surprising that Oliver was such an attractive figure to the junior nurses. He did not behave in the least like a consultant! "You must pay for the thermometer, of course—and I expect you've already felt the rough edge of Nurse Brook's tongue for upsetting her trolley in the middle of the dressings round."

"It was an accident, Sister," Phyllida said defensively.

"Some accidents are avoidable," Ruth said firmly. "You've been in nursing quite long enough to know that so much commotion upsets the patients. I know you have a lot to do and it seems that you'll never get done but you must learn to hurry without haste, Nurse Sims— and that isn't the contradiction that it sounds. I shall say no more but shall be watching you very carefully. You may go."

"Yes, Sister. Thank you, Sister."

On a sudden impulse, Ruth called her back.

She said lightly and with a friendliness that she seldom used to the juniors: "I used to have just that problem with my cap until I thought of putting in the hairclips upside down. They won't slip, then. It's something to do with the force of gravity, I believe," she added, smiling.

Phyllida beamed her gratitude. "Oh, Sister—thank you! I'll try that!" she declared and hurried out on the happy discovery that Sister Challis was much more human that she had suspected.

Such a simple solution to an eternal problem, Ruth thought, remembering how much trouble her own cap had caused her until Sister Booth had given her that same word of advice and gone on to talk of the earliest days of nursing when caps had been tied with long strings beneath the chin, the origin of the strings that ward sisters wore so proudly on Founder's Day each year. Being given one's own ward was still called 'getting one's strings'. Hartlake was very proud of its traditions and very proud of its nurses, too. The juniors might be irritated by the insistence on clean aprons and straight caps and regulation shoes and decorum on and off duty but such things were most important when the public regarded Hartlake nurses with such respect and admiration and put so much confidence in their skills.

Ruth was proud to be a Hartlake nurse. She had been very happy at Hartlake and it had been the greatest thrill of her life to 'get her strings', her own ward. But, as she had told Oliver, she did not aspire to be Matron. She had never meant to devote her whole life to nursing. Even when the hope of marrying Neil had been shattered and she was sure that she would never love again, it had not really seemed so impossible that the stubborn dream of marriage and motherhood would never be fulfilled. She was surely not destined to dwindle into a replica of Sister Booth!

Yet already, at twenty-three, she could hear herself using exactly the same words and tone as Sister Booth

when she admonished or advised her nurses and sometimes, when she was being very firm with a recalcitrant
patient, it was just as though an approving Sister Booth
was standing at her elbow. She had been much respected
and universally disliked—except by the patients she had
treated with the loving tenderness that a woman usually
reserves for her children. The patients *had* been her
children, of course. Her whole life had revolved around
her ward and her work.

Ruth could see the same thing happening to her,
unless she married Daniel. And marriage to Daniel
would be just an extension of her life at Hartlake. She
would have one patient in her care instead of twenty-six.
She did not think that she could face such a marriage
without love for him—or other compensations such as
the children he could not give her.

She had told Oliver that she meant to marry Daniel.
But it had been a defensive and rather defiant claim—
and rather premature in view of the fact that Daniel had
not even proposed!

Watching for Oliver's car that evening, she ran down
as soon as she saw it turn into the narrow street. She had
been weak enough to go out with him despite all her
resolutions. She did not mean to create temptation by
being alone with him in the flat if she could avoid it!

The car was parked on Waterloo Bridge and they
strolled across to the south side of the river and the
gleaming Festival Hall. It was a beautiful evening with
the sun glinting on the water and they paused for a few
moments to watch the river traffic—a police launch
cruising downstream, a pleasure boat packed with sight-
seers as it made its way to Greenwich, a small rowing
boat manned by naval cadets from the Chrysanthemum,

the training ship on the Embankment. The Thames flowed beneath the succession of bridges that linked the north and south side of the metropolis, the great river that had been so much a part of London's history through the centuries.

Ruth sighed. "I love it, don't you? The river, I mean . . . so stately and sombre and somehow soothing. Those people on the boat seem to be having a good time. I quite envy them!" The sound of the river guide's voice, describing the landmarks en route with remarkable enthusiasm in view of the fact that he uttered the same words perhaps thirty times a day during the season, carried quite clearly on the evening air in a lull in the traffic which crossed the bridge behind them.

Oliver smiled down at her. Sometimes, as now when she was eager and excited, she seemed quite enchantingly youthful and it was difficult to reconcile the radiant girl with the cool, capable ward sister. Loving her, he was moved to tenderness and marvelled that a man could be within touching distance of his fate for so long without realising it.

"We could take a trip to Richmond or Kew one day if you'd like it," he said.

Ruth looked at him doubtfully. "Would *you* like it?" Mingling with a crowd of day trippers on a pleasure boat scarcely seemed his scene but she realised she did not know very much about him. Still, the little she had learned in the past week had endeared him to her unexpectedly.

He did not say that his one aim suddenly seemed to be to please and delight her to the best of his ability. He sensed she would shy from the sentiment. But it was how he felt and, he suspected, how he would always feel. He was abruptly and deeply in love.

"Why not? We could forget our advancing years and our dignity for a few hours. There isn't a lot of fun in a consultant's day, you know, thanks to starchy sisters who disapprove of *entente cordiale*." His dark eyes, twinkling, teased her gently.

They walked on and he took her hand and drew it into his arm. Briefly, she tensed, reluctant for even that small and harmless intimacy and then allowed her hand to rest on his arm. But she wished he would not make it so difficult for her to think of him with a level-headed impersonality.

It was a perfect evening. The crowded and expectant auditorium hushed in an instant as Levitovski walked on to the platform and the brilliance of the famous pianist's performance brought tears to Ruth's eyes with one piece and bubbling delight to her heart with another, the sheer pleasure of listening to music in the company of a man who shared her love and her sensitive appreciation of its magic made everything seem wonderful.

It was an emotional evening for her heart was too full and the need to love and be loved was much too close to the surface. She had never known the full force of Oliver's charm, felt the true impact of his warm and pleasing personality, until now. She understood why so many women had loved him and, sure that he had never loved any woman, she stiffened her resolution not to make the same mistake. But she would need to keep a tight rein on her emotions.

It was flattering that he seemed to like her, seemed to be attracted, however briefly. Flattering and very dangerous, she thought wryly. For he could not have a serious or lasting involvement in mind. He was not the marrying kind . . . and if his career thrust marriage on him eventually, as it probably would, then he would certainly look to the Hilary Longhursts of his acquaintance for a suitable wife. The plain and totally unsophisticated Sister Challis of Paterson could not and should not hope for anything else.

Besides, nothing would induce her to marry a man like Oliver Manning, she told herself firmly. His well-earned reputation was no recommendation for a husband! She would never have a moment's peace if she married a man who could not resist a pretty face or the chance of another conquest!

At the end of the evening, rounded off quite delightfully by supper at the intimate little restaurant in Soho that she had liked so much, Oliver took her back to the flat. She felt just a little uncomfortable, knowing it would be very pointed if she did not ask him in and wondering how she could keep him at arms' length if she did. He had behaved beautifully, never once referring in any way to the intimacy that she wished so desperately to forget while reminded at every turn, and seeming to have nothing more in mind than her enjoyment of the evening. He was much too nice, she thought unhappily and wished she did not like him so much, wished her wilful body would not yearn for him so.

"Forgive me if I don't come in for coffee," he said lightly as he halted the car outside the house, solving the problem. "I have a deal of paperwork to get through tonight and I'm operating early in the morning." He smiled at her, the car's engine still ticking over, his hands resting lightly on the steering wheel.

He did not even mean to kiss her, Ruth realised with disappointment. "Another time," she suggested brightly and wondered if there would be another time. For she must be very disappointing to a man with his strong sexual appetite—and there were so many other women in the world. "Thank you for a lovely evening. It's been quite perfect," she said, not quite steadily.

"My pleasure," he said, meaning it. He ached to hold her in his arms and would not even put out a hand to touch her. He loved her—and she was possibly the only woman he had ever known who stubbornly refused to love him.

He leaned across to open the car door for her. She shrank into her seat as his arm brushed her breasts. He did not seem to notice but a little shadow swept across his handsome face.

CHAPTER EIGHT

Ruth straightened the crumpled coverlet and adjusted the pillows to make Mrs Hobbs more comfortable. The young woman had made a swift recovery from her ovariectomy with all the resilience of youth and hope for the future and now she was looking forward to being discharged very soon.

"Would it be all right to ask the doctor?" she asked anxiously. "I mean, if he'd just give me an idea. Laurie wants to arrange his holidays so we can go away. I mean, I feel all right, Sister, and I have healed up nicely, haven't I?"

"You're doing very well, Mrs Hobbs. I expect you'll be able to go home very soon. We'll see what Mr Manning says," she told her soothingly. She knew there was a very slight risk of a recurrence of the infection that had delayed her operation and it was for that reason that the girl had not already been sent home.

She moved on down the ward, pausing to alter the position of a patient's drip so that the saline flowed more smoothly. Mrs Mahadi wasn't so well this morning. After rounds, she would organise her removal to a side ward, away from the disturbing bustle of the main ward. The Indian woman was so slight and frail that her body scarcely showed beneath the bedclothes. Morphine eased her pain but she was a very sick woman. Ruth was worried about her for she had nursed enough Asians to know that they had little resistance to illness. This woman, like so many others, would not *fight*. All her life, she had accepted whatever was meted out to her without complaint—marriage at thirteen to a man she did not know, a succession of weakly children, poverty—and now the sickness that was slowly destroying her. Professor Wilmot had operated· and found that it was much too late for curative surgery. She had been returned to the ward and there was nothing they could do but ease the pain and discomfort of the last few days. Knowing little English, Mrs Mahadi scarcely spoke . . . and Ruth thought wryly that the women of her race did not seem to know how to complain.

She stooped to pick up a box of coloured tissues that had slid from the bed of the next patient.

"She's in a bad way, isn't she, Sister. Poor soul," Mrs Hay said in a piercing whisper.

"She's going to be fine, Mrs Hay," Ruth said briskly and put the box of tissues on the locker beside the bed, having a little trouble to find a space among the hotch-potch of personal possessions.

She continued her inspection of the ward in readiness for rounds. Oliver Manning was due with his students. Her heart quickened, a little foolishly. It was most un-wise to allow him to haunt her thoughts, she told herself sternly—and glanced once more at the neat little watch she wore on her wrist.

She had not seen or heard anything of him since the night of the concert. Having been called to a Sisters' Conference in Matron's office, she had missed his round earlier in the week and either lack of time or inclination had kept him from getting in touch with her. She remembered that he had left her that night with no mention of seeing her again and could not help wondering if it had been deliberate. She knew how fickle he was, how swiftly he lost interest. For some reason, he had kept his promise to take her to hear Levitovski. But he had not promised anything else.

She ought to know better than to believe that someone like Oliver could be seriously interested in her, she scolded herself, and then remembered with painful clarity the warmth in his smile, his flattering attentiveness, his unmistakable enjoyment of the evening they had spent together.

Had she been too pushing? She tried to remember every word she had uttered, every move she had made throughout that evening. He was the kind of man who would extricate himself swiftly if a woman seemed to be taking his interest for granted, she told herself wryly.

It was odd, a little disconcerting, that he had not so much as telephoned her throughout the week. But he was a very busy man, she tried not to think that he might have been busy with someone like Hilary Longhurst . . .

"Nurse Sims! Remove that trolley—*at once*!"

The horrified tone sent the junior scuttling to remove the offending item, left to stand by the swing doors of the ward. Ruth shook her head at the girl in mild exasperation. She did not seem to improve at all, she thought wearily. The girl was not only clumsy but scatterbrained!

Her heart leaped as the doors were pushed open on a flurry of white coats. Annoyed by the instinctive and most unprofessional reaction, it was a moment or two before she realised that the leading white coat did not belong to Oliver. Roger Pelling, his senior registrar, was preceding the group of students into the ward and was apparently taking the teaching round that morning.

Ruth choked back an absurd disappointment. But where was Oliver? He was not ill or she would have heard, she assured herself, as she moved forward to greet the surgeon. "Good morning, Mr Pelling."

"Good morning, Sister."

He had a very pleasant smile but it lacked that alarming power to melt all her resistance, Ruth thought, and wondered how she had come to be so involved with Oliver Manning in so short a time. She was just as weak and foolish as all those other women who had briefly enjoyed his interest. Why should she suppose that she was any more important? He had described her as a weakness—but it was very likely that he had already overcome it, she told herself firmly. She should be just as sensible!

She accompanied the group on the round, as usual. Mrs Hobbs was delighted to be told that she might go home as soon as her husband could make the necessary arrangements. Most of Oliver's patients were post-operative and doing well. Two new admissions were listed for surgery that day, both straightforward hysterectomies.

Being mainly routine, the round was finished quite quickly. Ruth walked to the swing doors of the ward with the registrar as etiquette demanded. "That woman is grossly overweight," he said impatiently, referring to the last patient. "My boss will have to plough through layers of fat to find the uterus!"

Ruth glanced up swiftly, a hint of betraying colour in her cheeks. "He will be operating, then? I didn't think he was here today."

111

"He's busy with an emergency Caesarean on Marie Celeste. That's why I'm taking the round this morning. But he'll look in later, I daresay. He likes to have a word with his patients before they go to Theatres, doesn't he?"

Ruth nodded, wishing her heart would not lift so ridiculously at the mere thought of seeing Oliver. What was the matter with her! It was just a silly infatuation, an absurd and deplorable physical attraction that had already wreaked too much havoc in her orderly life.

As it happened, she did not see him. He paid a brief visit to the ward and examined his two patients while she was at lunch, having left Jessica Brook to cope in her absence. Ruth had been very firm with herself and left the ward at her normal hour but she only toyed with the excellent food that was served in the sisters' dining-room. She seemed to have very little appetite of late . . . and little on her mind but Oliver Manning.

She had never liked or trusted him. Now, with very little reason, she liked him far too much. It would not do, she told herself sternly. The man had proved once more, at her expense this time, that he was just a rake and something of a rogue where women were concerned. He was a charmer, an experienced flirt with a glib tongue and smiling dark eyes and an undeniable talent for making a woman feel that she was the only one in the world for him.

She should have been firm with him at the very beginning and refused to be flattered by an interest that had proved to be as short-lived as the rest. After all, she had known how unlikely it was that she could really mean anything in his life.

But he *had* taken her to that concert, she thought

112

wistfully, tempted to think well of him. He had not walked away without a backward glance as soon as the conquest was made, as she had half-expected. He had given her a really wonderful evening—and that had done more damage than anything else. For she had found that there was more to Oliver Manning than a physical magnetism and a very persuasive charm that undermined a woman's resistance in no time. He was more than just an experienced seducer, an ardent and expert lover. Her heart had undoubtedly begun to respond to him as readily as her newly-awakened body—and that really alarmed her. For one experience of heartache and humiliation was more than enough for any woman. She must not fall in love with a man who was not at all likely to love her in return!

Returning to the ward, she learned of his visit and prompt departure and could not help wondering if he had timed the examination of his patients at an hour when he must know that she would be away from the ward. Perhaps he was avoiding her, but that was not the easiest thing for a consultant who had so many patients on Paterson, she thought dryly.

"Has that patient had her pre-med, Staff?" she demanded sharply.

"Yes, Sister. She'll be going down in a few minutes." Jessica Brook was a little surprised by the tart tone.

"Then why is she wandering about the ward? Get her into bed immediately and tell Nurse Sims to put her into a fresh gown and socks. Those are no longer sterile! No excuses, Staff!" she snapped as Jessica opened her mouth to explain that the woman had pleaded to use the bathroom and obviously slipped out when her back was turned rather than wait for a bedpan. "You know the

113

routine as well as I do. Even a first-year nurse knows better than to let a patient get up after a pre-med! Why is it that I cannot turn my back for ten minutes without the whole place going to pieces!"

"I'm sorry, Sister." Jessica hastened to usher the stubborn Mrs Gardner back into bed to await the porters who would take her along to Theatres. She ought to have kept an eye on the woman after giving her the injection to calm her natural anxiety before an operation. She had sent Nurse Sims for a bedpan and promptly turned her mind to other tasks.

But what was upsetting Sister Challis, she wondered, puzzled. She had never known her to be so sharp-tongued or to jump on the juniors as swiftly as she did of late. She had always been very capable and efficient and her sweetness of temper and equable moods made her one of the most popular sisters at Hartlake. She had been really edgy that morning, most unlike herself, fussing over trifles. She had even rebuked Mrs Hay for the untidiness of her locker top and the disorder of her bed. Jessica had never known her to speak so sharply to a patient.

If it had been any other girl, Jessica would have lightheartedly assumed that she was having touble with her love life. Hartlake had frequently been described as Heartache Hospital throughout her years of training, but it was common knowledge that Ruth Challis took no interest in men—which was kinder than declaring that the men were just not interested in the quiet, rather reserved and far from pretty sister in charge of Paterson Ward!

Lester had liked her, though. He had even taken her for the occasional drink. At one time, Jessica had even been just a little jealous, wondering if there was more to that friendship than appeared on the surface. But Lester was so kind and so good-natured. He took the trouble to get to know people, she thought tenderly, very thankful that he had not been deterred by her many put-offs and that stupid insistence that she loved Clive Mortimer rather than himself.

She had fancied that Ruth was very fond of Lester. But she had been so genuinely pleased when they announced their engagement and was so warmly interested in all the details of the wedding, planned for next month, that it was just not possible that her present mood was born of disappointment in that direction.

She looked into the office some minutes later as Ruth put down the telephone, having just been informed by Accident and Emergency that a new admission was on her way to the ward.

"May I go to have a meal, Sister?"

"Has Mrs Gardner gone to Theatres yet?"

"Just . . . and I've finished the drugs round."

"Oh, that's good." She made a swift, mental review of the nurses at her command. "Yes, you'd better go now, Staff. We've an emergency . . . a girl thrown off her moped. But we can manage without you, I think."

"Yes, Sister. Thank you, Sister."

Ruth hesitated. Then she said as Jessica reached the door: "Sorry I snapped at you, Jess. I'm feeling a bit fraught today."

Jessica smiled at her suddenly, warmly. "Oh, that's all right," she said. "Time of the month?"

Ruth, startled, glanced at the calendar and abruptly wondered that she had not noticed the absence of something as regular as clockwork. Too much on her mind, obviously.

115

"Yes," she said absently, untruthfully, a little sick dismay rising in her breast. Oh, it could not be! It was just one of those odd tricks that nature played from time to time. Hadn't she heard that the first sexual experience could interfere with the cycle . . . or was that just an old wives' tale?

She refused to panic. A few days was nothing to worry about, she told herself firmly. It was much too soon to suppose that she was pregnant—and surely she could not be so *unlucky*, she thought with a sudden desperation known to women throughout the ages.

In the ensuing bustle of the arrival on the ward of the young girl who had gone directly to Theatres from A and E, there was no time to worry. But the little anxiety remained at the back of her mind.

On her way to tea, late in the afternoon, she saw Oliver in one of the corridors, talking earnestly to a man she did not know. Her heart bumped and then she was suddenly, icily furious. For if she was pregnant, then it was entirely his fault and she did not doubt that he would treat her as cavalierly as he had treated her friend all those years ago. Her whole life would be in ruins, thanks to his stupid irresponsibility and his careless disregard for the consequences of his selfish and entirely sensual attitude to all women!

Oliver smiled, half-turned, ceased to listen to the excellent theory that was being so cleverly expounded by his colleague. Ruth looked through him with cold disdain and walked by. He had seen those green eyes sparkling with anger. He had never known them to hold so much glittering contempt. He was shaken. What had he done to merit *that* look?

The sin of omission rather than commission, he

thought wryly. She felt that she had been used and then abandoned like too many before her—and his reputation did not encourage her to trust him!

"Excuse me . . ." He left Anders in mid-flow, hurrying after Ruth to catch at her arm, uncaring that heads turned curiously or that there was unmistakable urgency in his unconventional use of her first name.

She turned, angry. "Really, Mr Manning!" The icy rebuke did justice to Sister Booth's teachings. She drew her hand from his arm with pointed dislike.

"I know," he admitted with rueful laughter in his dark eyes. He refused to be hurt or deterred by the manner which was surely only dictated by etiquette, long tradition. "I'm breaking rules again. I'm not a conformist, I'm afraid. I'm glad we ran into each other, Sister." The liquid warmth in his voice turned the formal address into an endearment. "My luck has really been out this week. Each time I've been to Paterson you've been off duty or elsewhere!"

"I daresay Nurse Brook has stood in for me perfectly well," she said briskly. "She's an excellent nurse."

He smiled down at her. "I've no complaints on that score. But I wanted a private word with you, Ruth."

She did not point out that he knew where she lived and her telephone number and that they need not be dependent on chance meetings in a professional capacity. "Yes?"

She was not encouraging, he thought ruefully. He was in her bad books—and all because he had chosen not to rush her, to give her time to make up her mind how she felt about him. He had swept her into bed—and regretted it to some extent. For he had meant their relationship to be conducted on very different lines to those he

117

had known with other girls. Ruth was very different. She was the woman he meant to marry—no, *hoped* to marry, he amended swiftly. For that easy arrogance belonged to the past. He had been humbled by a very real and lasting love and could only hope that Ruth might be persuaded to love him with time.

"Not here," he said, a little impatiently, conscious of the mill of people in that busy corridor, knowing that they drew attention, curious glances. "Are you busy this evening?"

"Yes, I am." Her tone was uncompromising.

"Tomorrow?"

"All the tomorrows," she said firmly, her chin tilting.

It was an unmistakable and quite final rebuff. He looked at her, disappointed and dismayed. She looked back at him, proud and a little defiant. Then she brushed past him and hurried along the corridor, not looking back. He was not likely to ask her again, she thought, relieved and utterly miserable, and wondered why she had felt suddenly sorry for a man who had so little real thought for her that he only remembered her existence when they bumped into each other in a hospital corridor!

Oliver was angry and sick at heart. There had been a frightening resolution in her eyes and voice and manner. She had really meant those cold words. She was not a flighty girl, playing hard to get. Ruth was mature and level-headed and she did not mean to be swayed by the looks and the charm that had won him any woman he wanted in the past. It seemed that she had relented in her long-felt dislike and distrust just long enough to captivate him completely—and then decided that she wanted no more of a man who could not compare with the Neil she had loved or the Daniel she was threatening to marry.

118

He loved her. But he could put her out of his mind and heart if he must. Only a little more of her strange and unexpected enchantment and he knew it would have been quite impossible. But perhaps the break had come at just the right time—and there were plenty of women in the world to console him, he told himself, whipping up anger to stifle the hurt.

Ruth absently rotated the plastic spoon in her cooling tea. Her anger was cooling, too. She had been horrid to Oliver because of that inner anxiety, that little panic that kept rising within her. But it was not fair to heap all the blame on him. She had been irresponsible, too. She had always known what he was and yet she had gone readily into his dangerous embrace. Perhaps she had nothing to worry about, she thought hopefully, and wondered if it was too early for a pregnancy test to give a definite result.

But supposing it proved positive! What on earth would she do? Tell Oliver, obviously—or would she? She knew how he would react to the news, she thought bleakly. Hadn't he denied all responsibility for Prue's condition all those years ago—and he had not even been a consultant then! The scandal would rock Hartlake to its foundations—a ward sister and one of its senior surgeons!

"You look washed out," Gillian Leigh told her bluntly, joining her at the small table. "It must be hectic on Paterson." She was the sister in charge of Marie Celeste, a lively and attractive girl with a mass of beautiful red hair and eyes that were so dark a blue as to be almost violet, fringed by long thick lashes. She jollied all the mums into having their infants with the minimum of fuss and bother and she was at her happiest with a

119

nursery of newborns to look after.

"It is," Ruth said with feeling.

"I expect you need a holiday," Gillian said sympathetically.

Ruth smiled thinly. "I've just had one." A fortnight with her mother in the Cotswolds, almost forgotten.

"Did you hear about our prem? Just two pounds and beautiful. He's doing as well as can be expected in an incubator, thanks to some very prompt work by Oliver Manning. We almost lost him *and* the mother this morning. Do you know, I've never seen anyone perform a Caesarean with such speed or such skill! That infant entered this world in the twinkling of an eye."

"He's a good surgeon, certainly." Ruth wondered at the irony of this particular colleague choosing to sit down with her to drink her tea. For everyone knew that she had a soft spot for Oliver. Gillian's name was on the long list of his conquests, she thought wearily, quite able to understand the attraction between them if not its abrupt but totally predictable ending.

She looked at the girl, admiring that unconscious loveliness and the confidence that she possessed in such measure, and refused to think of her in Oliver's arms. But had he called her *darling* when they embraced on the tide of passion, she wondered bleakly . . . and thought how unlikely it was that the poised and sophisticated and very attractive Gillian should ever become pregnant because of a moment's folly. Unlike herself, she would guard against such an eventuality. And, if it should happen, she would know just what to do. For a moment, Ruth toyed with the idea of asking for advice—and then dismissed it. For Gillian's wide-eyed incredulity that any man had taken so much interest in someone so plain and dull would be much too humiliating.

"*Good!* He's quite brilliant, my dear!" She eyed Ruth, a little curiously. "I wonder why you don't like him. You never have, very much."

Ruth shrugged. "I don't dislike him," she said coolly, carefully, as she had said to Daniel. "I just don't know him particularly well. We've never had much to say to each other."

"Well, you aren't his type, I suppose," Gillian said outrageously, meaning no offence. She grinned. "Count your blessings, ducky. Our Oliver has left a trail of broken hearts behind him. It will be interesting to see if marriage makes any difference to his way of life."

"Marriage?"

"Don't you know? He's engaged to Hilary Longhurst, the girl he brought to Founder's Ball. It's all over the hospital." Gillian did not know if the rumour had any basis in fact but she did not bother too much about accuracy when she was in a position to pass on an interesting piece of news.

Ruth's heart seemed to stop with the shock of the words. She did not think of doubting them. It seemed only too likely that Oliver could be engaged to one girl while amusing himself with another from what she knew of him. It was even in character that he had not mentioned his engagement to the Governor's daughter. Unless he had assumed that she knew. It was all over the hospital, Gillian had declared—but Ruth did not encourage her nurses to gossip in her hearing.

It was no longer so puzzling that he had not been in touch with her all that week. Just as she had supposed, his time and his attention had been taken up by his beautiful fiancée. She was deeply thankful that she had

121

snubbed him so mercilessly, left him in no doubt of her indifference and contempt.

She pushed away her untouched tea. "I must get back to the ward," she said with commendable composure. "I hope your prem gets on all right."

"Come up and see him some time," Gillian suggested, as proud as any mother.

"Yes . . . yes, I will." Ruth smiled stiffly and hurried away as the pain that had been stifled by shock suddenly welled to the surface.

CHAPTER NINE

Ruth put her hand on Daniel's shoulder and bent to kiss his cheek, as usual. Instantly, his big hand came up to cover her slender fingers and he turned his head so that their lips met.

She was startled and a little dismayed for he had never done such a thing before. She would not stiffen or jerk away for that must hurt him. But she did not allow her lips to linger. The pressure of his mouth, seeking a new kind of intimacy for their relationship, reminded her of Oliver's kisses. She felt oddly guilty as if she had betrayed Daniel. Yet she did not owe him any loyalty, she told herself firmly.

"How's everything?" he asked. His tone was light but his glance was searching. For there was something different about her, some change in her that he could not immediately define. Then he realised that she was not at ease with him. For the first time, he had the impression that she had come to see him out of duty rather than pleasure.

Well, that was very natural, he decided, forcing back the engulfing tide of pain and dismay. For why should an attractive young woman wish to spend her leisure hours with a cripple? She ought to be dining and dancing with a man who could give her all that a girl wanted. He was only half a man. Ruth deserved better . . .

"Fine—just fine." She smiled at him warmly, with affection.

"I thought you might not be coming, after all." The words and tone were too casual to be a reproach.

"I am late," she said ruefully. "The train broke down and we were stuck between stations for twenty minutes."

"No obliging consultant with a car this evening, obviously."

"No such luck," she agreed lightly but a tell-tale flush rose in her small face, immediately observed. "I ought to invest in a car of my own, I suppose. But there's so much traffic on the roads these days and I see the results of so many accidents . . ." She broke off, horrified, her face flaming at her thoughtless lack of tact. "I'm sorry, Daniel," she said, instantly penitent.

He reached for her hand, patted it gently. "I'm past being sensitive—and I don't want you to feel that you have to watch every word you say. You can always say anything you like to me, Ruth. We're friends."

"Oh, much more than friends!" she declared impulsively, lifting his hand to her cheek, truly sorry to have spoken so heedlessly. She would not hurt him for anything in the world.

"Well, I hope so," he said quietly. "I think you must know how I feel about you. I don't know how I'd have survived without you, Ruth. Life wouldn't have been worth living these last two years, believe me."

She was deeply moved. "Daniel, I've done nothing," she protested, feeling that she could have done so much more.

"You've kept me sane," he told her fiercely. He gripped her fingers so tightly that she almost cried out with the pain. "If things were different—if I had anything to offer you . . !" He broke off, choked with emotion.

In a moment, she was on her knees beside his wheelchair, arms about him, soothing and comforting him with wordless murmurs. For what could one say to a man who had so little and needed so much? "Dear Daniel," she said tenderly, very fondly. For he was dear to her and they were the very best of friends.

He rested his cheek on her bright hair, desolate. "I love you."

There was no joy for either of them in that quiet utterance. But it had to be said for the sake of his peace of mind.

"I know." Her heart ached for him because she could never, never love him.

Sylvia Seaton stopped short on the threshold of the studio, teacups rattling on the tray she carried. At the sight of that tender tableau, her heart had leaped with joy that a cherished hope was finally fulfilled. "Oh dear!" she exclaimed lightly, happily. "I didn't mean to interrupt . . . oh, bless you both!" Eyes filling with tears of relief and thankfulness, she hastily set down the tray and held out her arms to her niece. "Ruth dear, this is a dream come true! I'm so *happy!* And I know that you and Daniel will make a perfect couple!"

Startled, dismayed, Ruth struggled to her feet with the aid of Daniel's strong hand. About to protest, to deny that swift and utterly wrong conclusion, she paused, her heart pounding and her thoughts moving swiftly.

Marriage to Daniel would be the perfect solution to the problem which might be growing steadily beneath her heart, she thought recklessly. She knew without a shadow of doubt that she could rely on his support and discretion. And Oliver need never know! That was the greatest comfort of all! She would not have to go to Oliver for advice and assistance, she thought proudly. Loving her, needing her as he did, Daniel would understand, accept, might even welcome the child as if it was his own—and why did the world need to know that it wasn't! They could be married almost immediately.

But supposing she was not pregnant, not in desperate need of a father for her child? Marriage to Daniel must still be the answer to the bleak misery that had occupied her heart ever since she had heard about Oliver's intention to marry another woman.

"You've got it all wrong . . ." Daniel began indulgently.

"I'm so glad you're pleased, Aunt Sylvia," Ruth said swiftly, over-riding his words. She went into her aunt's warm embrace and received the kiss that was so obviously both thanks and blessing. She turned to Daniel and smiled into the astonished blue eyes, the expression in her own warning him not to speak, to spoil things. "Daniel hasn't exactly asked me to marry him," she said lightly and with perfect truth. "I think I said yes before he had a chance to do so!"

"That's true," he agreed, a little dryly. He was stunned, incredulous, quite unable to believe in his good fortune. But if, miraculously, Ruth was ready and willing to marry him despite all the drawbacks of his situation, then he did not mean to dissuade her. For she was a grown woman who must know what she wanted from life. He did not suppose that she loved him except as friend and cousin. He suspected that she had never ceased to love the man who had hurt and disappointed

126

her so much. But she must have good reason for failing to disillusion his impulsive mother—and he was glad enough to accept without too much question.

Sylvia kissed her son and then wiped tears from her eyes. "I don't know why I should be crying," she gulped, laughing at herself. "But I never really thought . . . it was just a dream . . . you're so proud, so independent, Danny!" It was years since she had called him by the childhood dimunitive. "Oh, this calls for a celebration!" she declared joyfully, so delighted that she scarcely knew what to say or do first.

"Pour the tea then, Mother," Daniel said, smiling at Ruth. He caught her hand and held it very tightly. "It will taste just like champagne as far as I'm concerned!"

While his mother poured tea with hands that shook, all a-tremble with excitement, Ruth bent down to Daniel. "We seem to be engaged," she said gently. "Do you mind?"

His eyes were very warm, very tender with the love that suffused his entire being. "Mind! It's what I've wanted for a long time. If *you* are sure . . .?"

"I'm sure," she said firmly, her heart almost failing her for she heard an echo of Oliver's voice, saying so gently, so tenderly: '*Sure, Ruth* . . .?' How gladly she had opened her arms to him without even knowing that she loved him. Looking back, she knew that it was only because she loved him that she had found so much joy, so much ecstasy in his arms. Love could come in a moment. She did not know when or how or why . . . and she had been obstinately blind and deaf to the truth until she had been shocked into awareness by Gillian Leigh's light announcement of his marriage plans.

It made no difference that he was a rake and a rogue with lying eyes and tongue and that any woman's love was wasted on such a man. She loved him for the kindliness and the tenderness he had shown to Miss Mallow among others. She loved him for the warm thoughtfulness that had led him to procure tickets for the Levitovski concert and the generosity of spirit that had shown itself when he took her to hear the great pianist and gave her a wonderful evening although she had treated him coldly. She loved him for liking the same music and sharing her sense of humour and being such a delightful companion as well as a perfect lover. She loved him.

It was loving such as she had never felt for Neil. That had been the love of a young girl, near to idolatry, bearing little relation to real and lasting love that was a perfect blend of the spiritual, mental and physical. Her love for Neil had been all in the mind, she thought wryly. Her love for Daniel could never be anything but spiritual, comfort and companionship for them both . . .

Donald Seaton was as delighted as his wife and the evening was spent in making all manner of plans. There was no question of Daniel and Ruth moving into a house of their own, of course. The extension to the family home, carefully designed and built to provide all the needs for a disabled man, was quite spacious enough to absorb Ruth and no one would be inconvenienced by her presence. There was no reason why she should give up nursing unless she wished. The local hospital would be only too glad to employ a Hartlake nurse with her qualifications and experience and it was only a matter of ten minutes walk from the house. They could be married in the local church where Daniel had been baptised and confirmed and no one would be more pleased than the vicar who called regularly to see Daniel and enjoyed long and intelligent discussions with him on a variety of subjects. No one would expect the wedding to take place in the Cotswolds in the circumstances . . . and surely Ruth's mother would understand?

No one noticed that Ruth took little part in all the eager planning. Happy and excited, it was enough for the Seatons that she nodded and smiled and raised no objection to all their suggestions.

She was committed and she did not mean to go back on her word. But nothing in the world could make her heart rejoice at the thought of marrying Daniel. So what did it matter when or where the wedding took place or where they made their home? As for the nursing career that had played so important a part in her life, it seemed very likely that it would have to be set aside for the more important career of motherhood anyway, she thought bleakly, and wondered when she was going to tell Daniel—and if there would be any need to tell him, after all.

The uncertainty was torment and while she dreaded confirmation of her fear, she felt that it must be better to know one way or the other. It would not affect her decision to marry Daniel.

When she eventually rose to leave, Donald Seaton instantly offered to drive her home and went to get the car out of the garage. Sylvia gathered up glasses and plates from the small celebration and went out of the studio with the piled tray.

It was the first moment that they had been alone since she had dragooned him into an engagement. Ruth moved across the room to him as he held out his hand.

"Are you *sure?*" he said again, searching her small face.

She smiled, squeezed his hand. "I shall begin to think that you're having doubts," she said lightly.

"Well, I am," he returned soberly. "Ruth, I've so little to give you."

"Oh, Daniel!" she protested gently. "You'll be giving me much more than you'll ever know!"

Comfort, companionship, a little consolation, rescue from the lonely years without love, the knowledge that she was needed for his happiness and, perhaps, love and security for another man's child.

He drew her down to the low cushioned stool, close by his chair, where she had sat for most of the evening. Keeping hold of her hand, he was silent for a moment, trying to find the right words.

"Ruth, you're a nurse," he said at last. "You've known plenty of people in my position. Some men are more fortunate than I am." He hesitated briefly, went on: "Able to enjoy sex with their wives, for instance. That isn't possible for me. I don't know if you realised?"

She carried his hand to her cheek. "I know, Daniel," she said quietly. "It doesn't make any difference."

He frowned. "You can't have thought, Ruth! You're young, attractive, a healthy girl. You're entitled to a proper husband, a normal marriage—and you must want children."

Now was the moment! But she hesitated—and the moment was lost. Suddenly she did not have the courage . . . not tonight. Perhaps when she was *sure*.

"There are lots of childless marriages that are perfectly happy," she said carefully. "And I *have* thought, Daniel. I want to marry you."

Clinging to a man who can't run away . . .

Oliver's words. Leaping to her mind, they sent an odd little shiver down her spine. For wasn't that just what she was proposing to do—and for that very reason? Daniel loved her. Daniel needed her. He could not play around with other women, hurting and disappointing her, making her afraid to trust him with her happiness, her heart.

He kissed her, very gently. The kiss of a cousin or a brother or a friend. A hint of things to come, the way it would always be . . .

It was impossible to sleep that night. It was warm, airless weather. Ruth threw open all the windows and wandered about the small flat in nothing but the flimsiest of silk wraps. Thoughts scurried round and round in her head like mice in a cage . . . and most of them seemed to be of Oliver rather than the man she was meaning to marry.

Her breasts ached for his embrace. Her wilful body yearned for the dear delight of his lovemaking. Most of all, she hungered for the sound of his voice saying *'darling'* against her lips . . . and wished with all her being that the tender endearment had come from his heart.

She must learn to live with the incessant ache of love and longing for Oliver, she told herself firmly. Just as the man she meant to marry had learned to live with the bitter gall of his shattered life. In doing what she could to make Daniel happy, perhaps she would find a measure of contentment for herself. She would be putting Hartlake and all its associations behind her for ever and in time she might cease to think of Oliver, to love him so much.

When she was very, very old, she might be able to forget the power and the glory in a man's passion and her own yielding and that brief, wonderful glimpse of a heaven on earth—when she was *very, very* old . . .

Ruth decided not to tell anyone of her engagement to Daniel for the time being. She had no particularly close friends at Hartlake and she had grown used to guarding her private life from curious eyes and ears.

She went quietly about her work, ensuring the smooth running of the ward, organising the daily routines, cheering and comforting the patients, teaching and advising her nurses—and no one suspected the turmoil of heart and mind.

When Oliver arrived for his round later in the week, she contrived to be busy with Mrs Mahadi in the side ward. She knew she could not avoid him indefinitely but she was not ready to face him just yet.

"I'll carry on here, Staff," she said briskly. "Go and attend to Mr Manning and make my apologies."

"Yes, Sister."

"Ask Nurse Trevor to come and help me. She can finish the fluid charts later."

"Yes, Sister . . ." Jessica went away and Ruth bent over the unconscious and very sick woman, carefully manipulating a feeding tube. The door was left open and she heard the murmur of voices. First Oliver's, quite unmistakable, and then that of her staff nurse, explaining. The group came along the corridor en route to the main ward and Ruth raised her head just as it reached the open door. Oliver glanced into the room and their eyes met. He did not pause and she continued with her work, scolding her heart for that quickening of response. Life would be very much easier when she left Hartlake and did not run the risk of seeing him at every turn.

Oliver did not allow that little anger inside him to

affect his attitude to the patients or the students. He was much too disciplined. He smiled, reassured, examined and explained, going about the round much as usual. He was aware of Ruth's comings and goings, her slight figure rustling about the ward, and wondered if she was only trying to be busy. She was much too organised and too able at delegating routine tasks to her nurses to have no time at all for dealing with consultants. Nurse Brook could be better employed than standing about with her hands behind her back or passing him a patient's chart or making the patient tidy and comfortable again after examination. She could be doing some of those menial chores that Ruth was apparently carrying out rather than accompany him on the round.

He found it strangely comforting that she wished to avoid him. It must mean that she was not so indifferent as she hoped to seem.

Moving away from a patient, his retinue of students hovering dutifully in the rear, he found Ruth in his path as she crossed the ward. He smiled and wished her good morning.

Ruth was compelled to pause, to return his courtesy with a brisk formality. She devoutly hoped that eyes and voice did not betray her. She tried very hard to whip up dislike for the handsome, assured and morally un-scrupulous man who had whisked her heart from her keeping without so much as a by-your-leave!

He kept her in conversation, discussing the condition of the grossly overweight Mrs Fletcher whose blood pressure had soared to quite alarming heights after the hysterectomy performed on her earlier in the week. She was on bed rest and sedatives and a special diet but the inaction after surgery was causing respiratory problems.

133

Ruth was anxious about the woman, too. In talking over the 'for and against' of getting Mrs Fletcher up and about, she forgot that he was Oliver, her dear love. He was a consultant surgeon and she was a ward sister and they had a mutual concern for a patient in their care.

It was agreed that Mrs Fletcher should be got out of bed and encouraged to take a few steps if the sphygmanometer registered a slightly lower reading that afternoon. "We'll see how she goes on," Oliver decided. "But I'm not at all happy about her, I must admit. Well, thank you, Sister. You've been most helpful . . . and I know just how busy you are this morning."

Ruth caught the hint of mockery behind the words. She looked up quickly. He knew that much of her busyness had been contrived. As always, those dark eyes saw far too much. He knew too much about women, she thought bitterly and almost hated him for it in that moment.

She managed a gracious smile that was Sister Booth to the life and glided away while he returned to his students and the round. She went into her office and sat down at her desk and busied herself with a list of drugs that were required from stock. But her heart was smarting with humiliation. He knew the impact of his unexpected attentions on her quiet and orderly and somewhat lonely life . . . and no doubt he knew just why she was running away from him. He had seen it all before.

As usual, she had left the door open so that she could keep an eye on the comings and goings in the ward corridor. But, head bent over her list and body tense with the effort to concentrate, to put Oliver out of her mind, she was not aware of him until he moved further into the room and touched her gently on the shoulder.

Ruth gave a start, dropped her pen as she turned in the chair.

Oliver stooped to retrieve it. "Sorry. I thought you heard my knock."

"No. I . . . I was miles away." Ruth clutched at the shreds of composure. She made no move to take the pen from his outstretched hand. She could not risk the swift response to his merest touch. After a moment, he laid it on the desk.

He looked down at her, clenching his hands in his pockets against an irresistible urge to reach out and draw her into his arms. She would not meet his eyes. She had no smile for him, no welcome, no encouragement. She did not seem the same girl who had gone so sweetly into his arms, given with such generous warmth and ensconced herself in his heart for ever . . . or the girl who had thrilled with him to the brilliance of Levitovski's playing and then walked hand in hand with him by the river, responding to him with shining eyes and a light heart, delighting him in so many ways.

"What made you suddenly put up the barriers, Ruth?" he asked quietly.

She stiffened. "I don't know what you mean—and I wish you wouldn't use my first name on the ward! Junior nurses seem to have twice the ears of anyone else and very long tongues!"

"Is that what bothers you? People talking? I thought we'd been very discreet."

"Discreet! With your car parked for all the world to see!"

He frowned. "So there is talk."

"Isn't there always talk about your affairs?" Her tone was tart, cutting, so that he did not notice the evasion.

She did not mean to mention his engagement to Hilary Longhurst if he would not! "I think you deliberately keep the gossips supplied. It lets a girl know that she isn't the only pebble on the beach and saves you a deal of explaining!"

Oliver raised an eyebrow. She was much too perceptive, he thought wryly. Those had been his tactics in the past. He could scarcely blame her for being so reluctant to trust him. But without trust, how could there ever be love?

"I should be delighted to believe that a dislike of being talked about caused you to snub me the other day," he said lightly. "I suspect it goes much deeper than that." He smiled suddenly, warmly. "I wish you would trust me, Ruth. I know my reputation is against me. But at least I've never left a girl standing at the altar!"

"No . . . and I shall be astonished if you ever get as far as the altar!" she flashed.

"For the first time in my life, I *do* have marriage in mind . . ." he began, knowing that it was not the time or the place for a proposal that would probably be unwelcome to her until she learned to trust him, to love him, but feeling that she might be glad of an assurance that his intentions were honourable.

"And so have I! You may be the first to wish me happy," she said brightly.

His eyes darkened abruptly. "What the devil does that mean?"

Her chin tilted at his tone. "It means that I'm getting married. Very soon. To Daniel. We're engaged."

"Madness," he said coldly. "Sheer bloody madness!" And he turned on his heel and walked out without another word, angrier than he had ever been in his life.

CHAPTER TEN

He brushed past Jessica Brook in the corridor without acknowledgment or apology. She looked after him, astonished. For whatever anyone might say about Oliver Manning, he was the most courteous of men.

She entered the office. "Whatever's the matter with our Oliver?" she asked curiously with the informality she only used when none of the juniors was in earshot. "He seems to be in a raging temper."

"I think I said something to upset him," Ruth said wearily. His words, confirming the rumour that he was to marry Hilary Longhurst, had pierced her heart.

"I should think you did! I've never seen him so put out—or put out at all, come to that! He's always so pleasant and even-tempered." But so was Ruth and yet she had been most unlike herself lately, Jessica thought shrewdly. Like any girl in love and looking forward to her wedding, it was tempting to look for signs of romance in the affairs of her friends. "I know it's none of my business," she said lightly, a little warily because Ruth did not encourage interest in her personal life. "But would you two have something going for each other, by any chance?" It seemed most unlikely. But there was nothing more unlikely than love, after all.

"No, we wouldn't—and I hope you won't go putting that idea into anyone's head!" Ruth said sharply. She hesitated. Then she went on firmly: "I didn't mean to announce it yet but I shall be leaving next month. Like you, I'm getting married." And heaven knew what would happen to Paterson and the patients without the two most efficient members of ward staff!

"But that's wonderful!" Jessica, liking Ruth, was really pleased. She was also astonished. "You're a dark horse, Ruth Challis! Why on earth didn't you tell anyone?"

"I told too many people the last time," Ruth said dryly.

"Oh!" Jessica had forgotten. "Oh, yes—well, nothing like that will happen this time," she said confidently. "Who is it? Anyone I know?" Her eyes widened suddenly, hopefully. "It isn't . . . it couldn't be *Neil!*"

"What a romantic you are," Ruth sighed. "No, of course it isn't Neil. I haven't seen him in years! It's a man I've known all my life." She chose to be evasive. She had not forgotten Oliver's mocking comments on the subject of her penchant for the familiar and safe. As if one could not love a man one had known since childhood just as much as a man one had only just met! She loved Daniel. Not as she loved Oliver, perhaps. But the eager, breathless excitement, the fierce need, the tender yearning would probably not last like the quiet, undemanding, comfortable and wholly reassuring affection she felt for Daniel. Marriage to Oliver wouldn't be a bed of roses for any woman, she told herself, and knew her heart contracted at the mere thought of his marriage to anyone else but herself.

Jessica saw that little shadow in the sister's eyes, and wondered. For a girl who was about to be married she was far from happy and, despite that swift, impatient

138

denial, she was abruptly convinced that Oliver Manning had been walking away from a lovers' quarrel. Who would have thought that Ruth, shy, reserved, outwardly so cool and level-headed, and Oliver Manning, rake and rogue and charmer that he was with an eye for the glamorous and sophisticated and exotic, might be lovers! What a turn-up for the book! And how infuriating that she liked Ruth too much to speak a word of it to anyone at Hartlake! The juiciest bit of gossip in many a long day and she was silenced by loyalty to a friend!

"I've told you in confidence, of course," Ruth said quickly. "I expect it seems very odd to you but I really don't want people to know. We are going to have a very quiet wedding with only immediate family and I don't want any fuss."

And that wasn't natural, Jessica thought shrewdly, even taking into account the hoo-ha of the last wedding that didn't come off. She herself went around advertising her happiness to all and sundry and boring anyone who would listen with wedding plans.

"I won't tell a soul if that's the way you want it," she assured her lightly. "Except Lester, of course. I'll swear him to silence, if you like."

Ruth smiled faintly. "That isn't necessary." She picked up the list of drug requirements and held it out. "Would you see that this list is taken down to Pharmacy straight away, please, Staff?" The formal address was an indication that the brief intimacy between friends was at an end.

Ruth rose and went to the window. The room seemed strangely airless and her head ached. Or was it her heart? She was just one mass of pain now that she had briefly allowed herself to give way to it.

She rested her forehead against the cool glass, staring down at the gardens without really seeing the green lawns, the bright flower beds, the imposing statue of Sir Henry or the usual milling throng. Yet she saw Oliver, picked him out immediately, sensing rather than seeing him at first. Tall, dark-headed, immaculate in the dark grey suit, swinging his lithe way across the gardens with a brief-case in his hand—and she saw the beautiful girl who moved to intercept him, auburn-haired, very slender, very elegant in the superbly-tailored trouser suit, unmistakably a Governor's daughter rather than a mere nurse! Meeting for lunch, no doubt, and what more natural for an engaged couple. The girl was a member of the League of Friends of the Hospital and it was spitefully said that it gave her every opportunity to attract the interest of the most handsome members of the male staff.

They met and paused and spoke and then, to Ruth's surprise, went their separate ways. Oliver did not look after the girl as one would expect and she did not turn back to smile and wave. They seemed to meet and separate like the merest acquaintances. Oliver just being unusually discreet, perhaps—but as the engagement had apparently been announced it seemed odd that they should pretend indifference in public.

As he neared the block that contained Paterson, he glanced up and unerringly found the window of her office. Ruth stepped back, but not before he had seen her and she was annoyed to have been caught watching him so obviously.

She hurried into the ward at the sound of crashing glass and found Phyllida Sims staring in dismay at a shattered and scattered vase of flowers that she had caught with her elbow as she plumped up Mrs Fletcher's pillows.

"Oh, you wretched girl!" Ruth flared, thoroughly on edge. "I really can't have you on my ward any longer! Clear up that appalling mess if you can do so without further disrupting the entire ward and then go off duty. You may expect to be on Matron's report in the morning!"

Phyllida flushed. She knew she was clumsy and constantly making stupid mistakes but there was no need for Sister Challis to speak to her in just that way in front of the patients, she thought rebelliously.

"I don't think you should speak to me like that, Sister," she said courageously. "We aren't servants, after all. I was clumsy and I'm sorry and of course I'll clear it up but . . ." She broke off, meeting ice in those green eyes and realising that she had committed the unforgivable sin of answering back.

"Go to my office and wait, Nurse Sims," Ruth said coldly. Sister Booth to the life, she thought, hearing her own awesome tones. "Nurse Blake! Clear away this mess, please." She went to the bed as Phyllida Sims hurried away, eyes filling with tears. She was much too emotional to be a good nurse, Ruth thought crossly and marvelled that the girl had ever got through her preliminary training. She finished plumping up the pillows and settled the big woman as comfortably as possible. "There you are, my dear," she said briskly. "It's a pity about your flowers but I expect Nurse can salvage some of the blooms and she'll find another vase."

"Don't be too hard on that little nurse, Sister," Mrs Fletcher pleaded in her hoarse, piercing voice. "She's a nice little thing . . . kind. I've got a girl at home just like that, can't turn round without knocking something over but she wouldn't hurt a fly, deliberate. Accident-prone, my husband says."

"Well, please don't encourage her to take up nursing," Ruth said humorously but with a hint of tartness. "We can't afford accidents in hospitals. There are enough going on outside for us to cope with!"

Phyllida Sims turned from the window as she entered the office, a mixture of fear and bravado in her eyes. Ruth sat down behind the desk. She did not invite the girl to sit.

"I am extremely annoyed with you, Nurse Sims," she said icily. "Surely you are aware that you undermine my authority with the patients once you begin to question it!"

"Yes, Sister. I'm sorry, Sister."

Ruth's eyes hardened. "You don't sound at all sorry." Her tone was tart.

"Well, I didn't like the way you spoke to me, Sister. After all, even a first-year nurse has some standing with the patients and to be treated like a wardmaid undermines that, don't you think?"

Ruth was silent, studying her. Then she said quietly: "Very well. I lost my temper. It's been a trying morning and that was the last straw, I suppose. I apologise, Nurse Sims."

"Oh, Sister . . . I'm sorry, too," the girl stammered, taken aback. "I really didn't mean to be rude and I do see what you mean about undermining your authority. It's just that I do feel that a Sister should be *fair* and you are, usually—and . . ."

"Very well, Nurse. That will do." As usual, Ruth found it necessary to cut her short. "Go back to the ward

142

and ask Nurse Brook to find you a quiet, safe job . . . sorting linen, for instance.''

"Yes, Sister. Thank you, Sister.''

As the girl went out, Ruth sighed and, resting her elbow on the desk, covered her eyes with her hand for a few moments. Thank heavens she had the afternoon off! She really needed to get right away from Hartlake and Oliver and exasperating junior nurses and Oliver and well-meaning friends and Oliver—if only for a few hours!

She stopped short at sight of the sleek silver car, parked outside the house. Her heart bumped . . . and then quickened with anger. What the devil did he mean by hounding her in this way?

She walked on, head high, temper barely under control. Oliver got out of the car as she reached it, smiled at her . . . and she walked past him and ran up the stone steps of the house, eluding his hand.

"Ruth!''

Angry, dismayed, he had needed time to cool down, to marshal his thoughts and emotions. Didn't he know just why she had run into the seeming sanctuary of Daniel's arms? Didn't he know that she was afraid to love a man who had apparently loved too many women to be loyal to one? Well, he loved her dearly and he could not imagine that he would ever want any woman but Ruth till the day that he died. All he had to do was convince her of that. It wouldn't be easy but by God! he meant to try!

She turned on him, angry. "What are you doing here? What do you want?''

He walked slowly up the stone steps. "You.''

She slotted her key in the lock. "Don't be absurd!''

143

He blocked her way into the house with an arm across the doorway. "It's your afternoon off, isn't it?"

She was surprised that he knew, wondered why he should have taken the trouble to find out. "So . . .?"

"Roger's doing my list this afternoon. I thought we could go for a drive—or for that boat trip on the river. It's a lovely day. The golden summer that the experts promised us, apparently. Will you?" Most unlike him, he was talking too much, being over-persuasive.

Ruth stared in amazement. Why did he want to take her out? Why had he opted out of his list that afternoon to do so? Why was he still pursuing her when he knew that she was engaged to Daniel and when the whole world knew that he meant to marry Hilary Longhurst? What did he hope to gain? She could not believe that she had anything to offer that he could not get very easily from a dozen other women!

It was just the thrill of the chase, she decided bleakly—the challenge in her refusals. If she stopped resisting, he would stop persisting, no doubt.

"I've a lot of shopping to do . . . a trousseau to buy," she said coldly.

He looked down at her ruefully. "There's a very obstinate streak in your nature, Sister Challis." He touched her cheek with his long, strong fingers. "Okay. So you're going to marry Daniel. It's your life. I hope you'll be very happy. But you aren't married to him yet. We could have this afternoon . . . just you and I, Ruth." His tone softened on her name, turned it into an endearment.

"Why?" she asked bluntly, steeling herself to resist the lure in his dark eyes, his smile, the touch of his hand.

His smile deepened. "Why not? Who gets hurt? There isn't going to be a lot of fun in your life once you're married to Daniel, you know. Have a little fun with me today, just for a few hours. Golden hours, Ruth. We won't talk about Daniel . . . or Neil . . . or Hartlake. Just us."

"What about Hilary?" she asked before she could stop herself.

"Hilary?" He laughed at the suggestion that she should feel any jealousy of a girl who meant less than any of the girls he had ever known. "No, we won't talk about Hilary, either. Just you and me."

His tone was low, coaxing. His dark head was very near to her own. Ruth's heart thumped in her throat. Golden hours . . . Just Oliver and herself, forgetting everything and everyone else, lost in the magic that he could create with his charm, his warm personality, his tenderness and his desire to please and delight. The power and the glory, she thought longingly, achingly, body melting in the heat of desire at the mere thought of his arms about her, his lips on her own . . .

"You're entirely without morals or conscience," she said slowly, scathingly. Grieving for the might have been, she struck out to hurt before one word, one gesture betrayed her love and her need.

His eyes darkened abruptly. He straightened his tall frame, took his arm from the door. "Well, that doesn't leave me in much doubt how you feel, does it?"

Turned to stone, Ruth watched him get into the car, turn on the ignition and drive off down the narrow street at top speed.

Shaking, she let herself into the flat. She did not cry easily. Some things went much too deep for tears, anyway. She sat on the edge of the sofa and gripped her hands tightly in her lap and felt as if she had sent away the only happiness that she would ever know in life.

Which was ridiculous when he did not love her and never would and meant to marry a very different kind of person to herself . . .

Oliver had swallowed his pride because he loved yet neither loving nor humility had come easily to him. It seemed that both were a waste of time and the sooner he went back to enjoying life with a succession of pretty and willing girls and forgot all about settling down for life with someone like Ruth Challis, the happier he would obviously be!

Let her marry the poor devil who was nothing more than a substitute for the man who had let her down. He could not prevent her from taking a wrong turning in life—and why the hell should he care! She was not the only woman in the world!

She was for *him*, Oliver admitted wryly. He had tried to give her love and tenderness. He had been ready to marry her, to devote his life to making her happy and giving her everything she could possibly want. He had persisted long after most men would have shrugged and walked away. It seemed that she did not want what he could give her. She meant to marry Cousin Daniel and put an end to the hopes and dreams, the love that possessed him like nothing else in his life.

Why Ruth? Why that one woman of all the many he had known? Why the only girl who had never liked or approved or trusted him throughout the years? And, most important of all, why had she relented and gone into his arms with such shy, enchanting sweetness and such generous, delightful response, capturing his heart in a moment? Meaning to marry Daniel—and she had really made no secret of it—why had she encouraged

146

him to love her? To seek an odd kind of revenge on one man for the crime of desertion by another? Or to punish him for that imagined hurt to her former friend? Women were the strangest creatures, he thought ruefully, a trifle bitterly.

Well, if she had set out to hurt him, knowing that he cared—and heaven knew that he had made no secret of that, either—then she had certainly succeeded. She had touched the very core of him with those harsh, contemptuous words. More than that, she had shown him how hopeless it was to hope.

The journey to Woodford had never seemed so long. Or was it only that her heavy heart found no comfort in the thought of the hours she would spend with Daniel and his parents? There would be more talk of the wedding, the future. Ruth wondered if she could bear it.

She thought wistfully of the river on that hot, oppressive afternoon. The river and Oliver by her side, his arm lightly about her shoulders or holding her hand as they walked along the towpath at Richmond after taking the river boat from Westminster Bridge. A golden afternoon . . . a few golden hours to remember. Was she a fool to have spurned the offer? Oliver had said there would be little fun in her life once she married Daniel and it was true, she knew. No concerts, no trips on the river, no visits to intimate little restaurants in Soho and no Oliver with the quick, sparkling wit, the lively humour, the engaging charm and the heart-warming attentions that sprang from a natural courtesy and kindliness.

Her heart rebelled at the thought of her future with Daniel. She would not be a wife but just a 'daughter of the house', caring for him, tending to his needs, sharing the household duties with his mother and talking domestic chit-chat, humouring his genial, talkative and hard-working father. For the rest of her life! It was unthinkable!

Then she remembered—and her heart sank. Surely it was more unthinkable that she should face a lonely and frightening future, pregnant by a man who cared nothing for her and would soon be another woman's husband! She must marry Daniel—and be grateful for a kind and loving husband, a good home, security and companionship throughout the coming years. Baby or no baby, she would still need Daniel to give her those things! She would never get them from Oliver!

Daniel was busy with a deadline to meet. He greeted her absently, his mind very much on his work. She stood and watched the quick, skilful fingers as they wielded the pencils—but only for a few moments. He found it distracting and said so, kindly but obviously anxious to be left alone to work.

Ruth wandered about the garden until her aunt should return from shopping. It was a very pretty garden, lovingly-tended by the green-fingered Sylvia Seaton, an occupation cultivated during the long years of neglect by a busy husband and an active, happy-go-lucky son. Since Daniel's accident, there had been less time to give to the garden but no doubt she was looking forward to more leisure once he and Ruth were married and she could shelve much of the daily burden, the responsibility and the work.

Ruth had little appreciation for the beauty or the heavy scent of the roses, the pretty and well stocked flower borders. She was restless, troubled in mind and spirit. Was this how it would always be, she wondered. Daniel spending most of his waking hours at the easel, needing to occupy his mind and justify his existence by working and earning—and herself trying to fill the long hours?

She must certainly apply for a job at the local hospital. She could not settle for this kind of boredom after the hustle and bustle of Paterson, the urgency, the knowledge that one was needed and that one's skills and long training were vital to the survival and recovery of the sick and the maimed.

Her career was just as important to her as Daniel's art was to him, she thought fiercely. She could not give it up so easily. Surely Daniel would not expect it of her? She remembered that he had frowned when his father mentioned the local hospital where she might work and said, rather pointedly, that there was plenty of time to think about that and he hoped there was no need for his wife to go out to work.

Daniel's life was so circumscribed that he might well resent a working wife, Ruth thought shrewdly. She would meet and mingle with people he did not know. She would move in a world in which he had no place. That was perfectly all right for a cousin, a friend. But not for a wife, perhaps.

A man in his position was usually proud, possessive, clinging, frightened of losing the little he did have. A wife who worked might meet another man who could give her all that he could not. Oh, Ruth perceived and understood—and wondered again if it would be wise to marry Daniel, after all. Better to be another Sister Booth with a full and busy life than a frustrated and bitter wife-who-was-not-a-wife in an ivory tower.

Then she remembered—and her hands clenched. How was it possible to keep forgetting something that

149

haunted her day and night, she wondered despairingly. Oliver's hard and urgent body against her own, Oliver's seed, Oliver's child growing within her . . . maybe! She ran her mind back over the days, slipping by at speed because they were so busy, dragging so dreadfully between dates on the calendar. It was too early for other signs of pregnancy, she knew. But surely it was possible to know *yes* or *no* at this stage.

Daniel manoeuvred his chair out to the terrace. Feeling oddly guilty about neglecting her when she had made the long journey to be with him for a few hours, he had thrown down his pencils and turned away from the easel. Marshall was waiting for the drawings but he could always work into the night. He did not sleep very well and the night was often spent in futile might-have-beens. He had perfected the art of swinging himself from bed to chair and often roamed about his part of the big house, entirely open-plan to his own design, or in the cool shadows of the garden when the world slept.

About to call to Ruth as she stood in a quiet corner of the peaceful and secluded garden, he saw that she slowly lifted her hands to cradle her abdomen in an age-old gesture and there was a strange look of mingled hope and anxiety on that small, sweet face.

Daniel abruptly realised just why she wanted to marry a man who had nothing to give but his name and the security of marriage.

He was not shocked, not even particularly dismayed. It was the explanation he had sought and it was more acceptable to him than the pity that did not spring from loving.

He was glad that Ruth had turned to him, sure that he would not fail her. He was glad that he could do so much for the girl he loved with all his heart.

150

CHAPTER ELEVEN

Oliver could not be anything but courteous, Ruth thought. It was not in his nature. But oh! the ice, the steely reserve for all his courtesy, his smiling deference, his pleasant manner. The smile did not reach the dark eyes that looked through her so coldly that her heart flinched. When he turned to her, spoke to her before his patients, his students, her nurses, he was very much the consultant addressing the ward sister for all his seeming friendliness, so unusual in a senior surgeon, so much appreciated by ward staff. His use of her title, carelessly formal, held not even the smallest hint of a caress any more. He left the ward as soon as the round was over, never finding the least excuse to linger or to return. He had nothing to say to her now that the whole world could not hear, Ruth thought miserably.

Her heart was breaking. She had supposed that she knew all about heartache, despair, broken dreams. But losing Neil had been as nothing in comparison. Because she had not seen him again since he left Hartlake, the disappointment and dismay had been gradually lessened as nursing became more important. But she was reminded of Oliver at every turn and knew that the love and the need would never grow less.

She had been little more than a schoolgirl when she loved Neil. Now, she was a woman and Oliver had awakened heart and mind and body to the real meaning of loving. Without him, life must be a desert, a void, a nothing—the mere filling of days with trivia.

Ruth supposed he would soon be married, but she had not heard and would not ask. At least the juniors were agog with rumours of a romance between the new Sister Tutor and Roger Pelling and Oliver's affairs seemed to be forgotten.

She did not know whether to be deeply thankful or sorry to find that she was not pregnant after all. Her cycle had simply missed a month—a kind of punishment for giving way to her impulses, she thought wryly. It was a relief, of course . . . and yet! A child would have been something of Oliver to love and cherish, she mused wistfully.

Sternly, she told herself not to be a fool. Many a girl would be grateful to escape so lightly from a foolhardy business. Now she would not have to confess to Daniel, pass off another man's child as Daniel's before the world. Now she could relax, forget the anxiety that had lain so heavily on mind and heart. Now she could really turn her thoughts to wedding plans and her future as Daniel's wife.

Now she need not marry him at all . . .

The thought came swift, hopeful. Ruth toyed with it, tempted, and put it aside. Daniel loved and needed her and she could make him happy—and what did it matter that she loved another man? He was going to marry Hilary Longhurst.

Despite the cold and hurtful indifference behind that charming smile, Ruth's numbed heart came alive when Oliver walked into Paterson. She took care not to be away from the ward or busy when it was time for his round. Her eyes scarcely left that handsome face as she stood demurely by, listening, observing, ready to answer questions or receive instructions—and longing for the ice to melt just briefly. It did not.

Like any little junior nurse in love and caring nothing for appearances or pride, she contrived to see him by making excuses to visit Out-Patients on his clinic days, chancing to be talking to Theatre Sister when he arrived for an afternoon's surgical list, calling him to the ward when a patient's condition gave the least cause for anxiety rather than coping or turning to his senior registrar.

Oliver did not seem to notice that she was cropping up in his life much more frequently than of old. But Ruth was sure that she was making a fool of herself, that he knew from experience all the ruses and shifts that a woman would go to just to spend a few minutes in his company. He did not give the smallest sign of responding or of relenting in his newfound dislike and disdain.

If he had cared at all—and surely he had!—then she had killed all interest, all liking, all desire with those insulting words. He was not a man to give second chances, she thought bleakly, a little despairingly.

Hurrying back to Paterson from a vain foray to Out-Patients in the hope of seeing him, if only for a moment, Ruth turned a corner and collided with him. She had been guilty of taking the corner too sharply like so many of her juniors who never seemed to anticipate that someone else might be doing exactly the same thing, she thought wryly, breathless with shock and leaping delight.

Oliver instantly caught her by the arm, steadying her. A little concern leaped to the dark eyes for he had been hurrying, too, late for his clinic—and she was so slight, so frail, so obviously winded.

"All right?" Wanting to say so much more, he was brusque.

"Yes—yes, of course. My fault!" She managed a smile for him, wondering if he knew that she trembled at the touch of his hand. It seemed a lifetime since her body had quivered in swift, sweet response to this man. It was an eternity of longing since those dark eyes had smiled with meaningful warmth and the hard, urgent mouth had lifted her to heaven with his kiss.

Oliver meant to walk on, having apologised, ensured that she was not hurt. But he hesitated. "I hear that you are leaving soon." Careful to keep all emotion from his tone, he sounded stony, indifferent. How much he had missed her! How much he wanted her! And how damnably difficult it was for a man when the woman he loved and could not have seemed to be here, there and everywhere in the busy hospital, haunting him with her bright hair and sweet face and trim figure, tormenting him with her unruffled coolness and wholly professional manner.

"At the end of the month," she agreed brightly, while her heart wrenched that he cared so little whether she went or stayed.

"Hartlake won't be the same without you," he said carefully. It was the kind of thing that anyone might say. He meant it with all his heart and wondered if she knew—and if she cared at all. As she was still so set on marrying Cousin Daniel, it did not seem that she did, he thought heavily.

"I shall miss Hartlake, of course." And *you*, her heart cried, so much more!

"That pretty nurse on your ward is leaving, too, getting married, I understand?" As if he gave a damn but

154

the empty conversation kept her for a few moments while he committed that enchanting face and the sweet mouth and the serious green eyes once more to memory.

"Nurse Brook."

"I expect so. I can never remember her name."

Ruth was comforted. She did not mind that he had noticed Jessica's prettiness for every man did! It would have hurt, though, if the girl's name had come easily to his lips.

"She's getting married next week," she said, wondering if he was interested in knowing the date of her wedding to Daniel, wondering when he would marry Hilary Longhurst. It seemed a little odd that no one was talking about his wedding plans. Oliver Manning's affairs had always been of so much interest to her fellow-nurses. One would have thought that his marriage would have caused more of a stir.

"We're losing too many of our best nurses that way," he said dryly and thought that they might all go and gladly if only Ruth would stay, within occasional sight and sound if not in his arms and playing an important part in his life. He seemed to live for those all-too-short encounters on the ward and about the hospital and the strain of keeping such a stern control on his thoughts and feelings was beginning to tell on him. Now, trusting himself not one jot further, he gave her a careless nod of farewell and went on his way.

Ruth returned to Paterson where she found a minor crisis and no one but herself apparently able to deal with it. It caused her to wonder dryly if Hartlake could afford to lose her at the end of the month. A foolish conceit, perhaps, but mentally reviewing her present staff she felt that, without herself and the capable Jessica Brook, the

155

patients would be left to the tender mercies of scatter-brains like Phyllida Sims!

An exaggeration, of course. Matron was aware of the problem and working on it. She would have a replacement for Jessica when she left and her own successor as ward sister would shortly be announced, no doubt. Ruth thought ruefully that she would be forgotten soon after her departure because, unlike Sister Booth, she had not been at Hartlake long enough to make an indelible impression on anyone—and least of all Oliver!

That evening, she began the oft-postponed task of sorting through her possessions. Someone was already waiting to take over the tiny flat when she left. Ruth felt that she would miss its privacy and the warm camara-derie of the other girls in the house, all nurses at Hartlake like herself. She did not look forward to mov-ing into that rather cluttered, pretty-pretty guest room in her aunt's house where she slept on occasional weekends. There was no question of her sleeping with Daniel. She would be nurse, companion, mother-substi-tute but never truly a wife, she thought, sighing.

It was amazing what she had acquired in the space of two short years! The pile of accumulated 'treasures' grew steadily—old letters, snapshots, postcards, theatre programmes, receipts, notes from friends or colleagues, various newspaper cuttings, recipes, birthday and Christmas cards. Ruth felt as though she was putting aside her youth with the small souvenirs.

Then she came across a programme for the Levitovski concert and she sat back on her heels, the tears suddenly stinging her eyes. A crumpled programme, stained with wine, was all that she had to remind her of that brief affair with Oliver. Knowing him throughout the years, it was all that she should have expected, she told herself bitterly.

But memory came crowding upon memory . . .

. . . Oliver, sitting on Miss Mallow's bed in disregard of conventional behaviour for a consultant, holding the old lady's hand and smiling with the genuine concern and warm friendliness that had always redeemed him in her eyes despite his rakish ways . . .

. . . An exchange of smiles at the end of a tricky operating session, a little surprise that he had been more aware of her throughout than she had thought and a sense of shared relief after shared concern . . .

. . . Dining with Oliver by candlelight, shy and unsure of herself and wondering if she ought to encourage the surprising interest of a man she had never really liked or trusted . . .

. . . The touch of his hand, laid gently against her cheek in unmistakable caress—and the first stirrings of response in a heart that had thought it could not love again . . .

. . . That first kiss, scarcely a kiss at all, with the heart-warming tenderness that had taken her into his arms so trustingly. . .

. . . The golden, glorious rapture that she would probably never know again . . .

. . . Listening to the brilliant Levitovski, her hand lying in Oliver's clasp, knowing a swift lift of her heart as the soaring beauty of the music filled the auditorium—unless it was a sudden awareness of loving that had made that moment so memorable . . .

. . . And the look in his eyes when he turned away, hurt and offended by her scathing words, finally rebuffed—and all because she knew that she was no more than a brief enchantment in his life like all the others before her . . .

Ruth wept a little. Then, resolute, she put the programme with all the other reminders of a past that had no part to play in her future.

In the morning, she retrieved it, smoothed it, placed it carefully among her personal papers. It was all she had of Oliver and she could not part with it. He had handled the programme, turned its pages with her, pointed out his favourites among the selection of pieces. Later, he had accidentally spilled some wine on it and dabbed it with his table napkin. At the end of the evening, he had watched her slip it into her bag as a souvenir, a little smile in his dark eyes.

The days that she had no hope at all of seeing him were long, dragging affairs and this was one of them. Remaining opportunities were pitifully few, for the end of the month loomed much too large and she had moments of panic when she thought of the wedding, arranged to take place in a register office in two weeks time.

Now she understood how Neil had felt as the date drew inexorably nearer and his feeling that he was doing the wrong thing grew stronger. It had taken a kind of courage to back out at almost the last minute, she thought, finally forgiving him. She knew she was a coward. She could not banish that look of love and trust and glowing happiness from Daniel's dear face or the thankful relief and delight from his mother's eyes without very good reason.

Her love for Oliver was no excuse at all, in the circumstances. For he did not love her, want her, or deplore her marriage to someone else. He had even given it his blessing, she remembered bleakly, more concerned with the well-being of a man he did not know than with her chances of happiness. His heart could be warmly compassionate towards a disabled stranger, completely untouched by love for her or any woman, apparently.

The thought of leaving Hartlake, of giving up the ward which meant so much to her, was very depressing. She would miss it all so much. Nursing had been her life, more important than anything, until Oliver had so unexpectedly filled her heart to overflowing with love and longing.

Travelling to Woodford that evening, a thrice-weekly event at the moment, Ruth wondered if she could continue working at the hospital on a part-time basis. She would not be able to remain as ward sister, of course. But she would still be part of Hartlake and would still see Oliver from time to time, she thought wistfully. But that would give her no comfort at all. For encounters with the man she loved would only emphasise the bleak futility of her life with Daniel.

She realised her negative approach to the future was very wrong, and hoped that Daniel did not sense her growing unease. But, if he had doubts, he did not voice them any more than she did.

It was a comfort to Daniel to realise that he could do something for Ruth, that he was not entirely a hulk of impotent masculinity. He could not give her a child but he could provide a home and happiness and security for the child she was carrying. She had not mentioned her condition to him. Knowing her as he did, it surprised him that she could not be completely frank with him. They were very close.

Nor was it like Ruth to cheat. But perhaps she felt, as

he certainly did, that he was getting the best of the bargain. He had not been trapped into anything against his will. It had been his dearest wish for some time to keep Ruth by his side for ever. That he had some other man to thank for her willingness to marry him did not really matter. The probability that she loved the man in question was not really important. It seemed that circumstances prevented her from marrying him and Daniel knew that she had a horror of abortion for the sake of expediency. In Ruth's book, if one made a mistake one should pay the price. Well, that was entirely to his advantage, thought Daniel, loving her and meaning to make her as happy as his limited powers would allow.

It was a wet evening and Ruth was caught in a downpour as she hurried from the station. When she arrived at the house, rain had dampened her bright hair and a cold wind had whipped colour into her small face.

As she shrugged out of her raincoat, Daniel regarded her with a welling of tenderness. "I'm glad to see you, of course. But you shouldn't have come out on a night like this," he said warmly.

Ruth laid her cold cheek against his own, very briefly. "A little rain won't hurt me. I'm not sugar and I won't melt," she said lightly.

He noticed that she was a little breathless. "You've been running."

She nodded, laughing. "Yes . . ."

"Not very wise."

Ruth glanced at him, surprised. "Wise . . .?"

"In your condition," Daniel said deliberately.

Her heart missed a beat. So he had *known*—and accepted without question or condemnation. But how

160

had he known? How could he possibly have known?

She drew the low stool closer to his chair and sat down. "Daniel, there isn't any 'condition'," she said quietly, carefully. She reached for his hand. "I thought there might be but it was a false alarm." She had to be absolutely honest with him, she knew.

"Do you want to tell me about it?" he asked gently.

She carried his hand to her cheek. "Not much to tell . . ." But she told him, naming no names, about the moments of madness, a man who did not care for her, the fear of 'consequences' and the impulse that had led her to turn to Daniel and her determination to make him happy.

He listened, very thoughtful, saying nothing until she had finished. Then he was silent, torn between the feeling that he should release her now that she had no need of a husband after all, and the selfish longing for the happiness that she could give him. Not once had she spoken of loving the man in question but he knew her too well to doubt that she did. Ruth was simply not the type to be swept off her feet by a Casanova. She had always been so 'touch-me-not', something of a prude and rather puritanical in her disapproval of the sexual laxity of the times—typical of a girl who had never been in love or experienced the full force of passion for any man.

Such a virginal air would be a challenge to a certain type of man, Oliver Manning, for instance. Daniel did not know him but he had heard Ruth speak slightingly of him and guessed that he had a reputation where women were concerned. He remembered a little consciousness in Ruth's voice and manner on a certain evening when Manning had not only dropped her off at the house on his way to visit a patient but also offered to take her home at the end of the evening. He was a consultant, apparently, an important personage in a hospital's hierarchy. Would he pay such unusual attention to a ward sister unless he was in hot pursuit?

It was a temptation to close his mind to the probability of her love for Manning. He loved Ruth, he needed her desperately, and she was not a child. She must know what she was doing. She had manoeuvred their marriage for a reason that no longer existed but she did not seem restless, unwilling, or at all unhappy about the future. No doubt she felt that it was futile to love someone like Manning. Or perhaps the man was married. However it was, she seemed content to marry him, Daniel told himself, and in time she would forget all about the other man. She might even come to love him. There was absolutely no need for him to offer to release her from their engagement.

"Still want to marry me, Ruth?" He spoke lightly but his hands tightened convulsively on the arms of his wheelchair to still their shaking. He felt sick with the pounding of his heart, the fear that rose to catch him by the throat. He could not bear to lose her, to see his happiness dashed from him at almost the last minute.

"Of course," she said quickly but her heart turned over at the thought of escape from something she dreaded more with every day that brought it closer. She loved Daniel dearly, but marriage? And such a marriage? She would be locked in an ivory tower! "What would I do without you?"

But Daniel's sensitivity had caught that tremor of hesitancy and it was enough. Swamped by pain and the bitterness of disappointment, he knew that he must not marry her even if she wanted it. For his lovely Ruth deserved so much better than the life he could give her, he told himself firmly. She should have a normal marriage and the eventual joy of children and he could not give her those things. She was warm and loving and sweetly generous and he realised she would sacrifice herself rather than go back on her word.

He knew that not one word of regret or reproach or resentment would ever be uttered in his hearing. But she would regret and she would resent for they were very human feelings—and in time she might even hate him a little for holding her to a promise made in affection and compassion and, no doubt, a little despair.

Loving her, he must set her free.

Needing her, he must travel that bleak road into the future without her, after all.

"You're a kind girl, Ruth," he said gently. "But it isn't the answer, you know."

She looked at him, raising a little hope and trying not to let it show. "I hope you don't mean to be noble," she said firmly. "Not being pregnant doesn't mean that I don't need you. That isn't why I wanted to marry you, Daniel." She added with her innate honesty: "It was *a* reason. It wasn't *the* reason."

He brushed a wisp of the chestnut hair from her brow, the touch of friend rather than lover. "I know the reason, Ruth. At least, I think I do!" She raised an eyebrow in swift query. He smiled at her gently. "You needed to feel safe, needed someone you could trust—and I wasn't likely to run away."

A little colour stole into her face. It was strange that he should use almost the same words as Oliver. To some extent, she supposed it was the truth. It had never occur-

163

red to her to doubt Neil and he had let her down. She had been afraid to trust any man since—and Oliver, least of all!

She *had* felt that she must be safe if she entrusted her happiness and her future to Daniel. But he was so much wiser than herself. He was brave, too, facing facts squarely and without flinching. He had been compelled to face a good many harsh facts in the last two years, she thought sorrowfully.

She did not doubt that Daniel loved her. Certainly he needed her. But she realised that he was ready to release her because he knew that the kind of happiness and the kind of future that she would find with him was not enough. He was setting her free to love and be loved like any normal girl. Not Oliver. She knew that could never be. But, perhaps, one day, someone else.

"I do love you, Daniel," she said sadly.

"As I love you . . . in the way of friendship. It would be a pity to spoil something so precious." He looked at her, very tenderly. "I should gain a wife and lose my dearest friend. Nothing would ever be the same between us, you know. I should always feel that I was failing you in so many ways—and you would always be afraid of seeming disappointed."

Ruth sat silent for a few moments.

Then she said, a little wryly: "So I am not to be married, after all, for the second time."

Daniel smiled and leaned forward to kiss her lightly. "Third time lucky for you, Ruth. I feel it in my bones . . ."

CHAPTER TWELVE

Ruth was thankful that only a handful of people had known about her engagement to Daniel. Before, it had seemed that the whole world knew she had been jilted and she had suffered accordingly. The reserve she had acquired since those days now stood her in good stead.

Matron was too delighted when she withdrew her notice to ask many questions. As she had not yet appointed a new ward sister to Paterson, no one was disappointed by Ruth's change of plans.

Jessica was in a whirl of excitement with her own wedding only days away and Ruth, doubting that they would meet again in the future, decided not to cast a damper by mentioning her broken engagement. As she had never talked very much about her affairs, it obviously did not seem strange to Jessica, full of her own plans, that Ruth had so little say about her forthcoming wedding.

She did confide in Theatre Sister. Plump and jolly and very popular, Liz Carter was the closest thing to a girl-friend that Ruth possessed. She could convey warm sympathy and understanding without words and she was not the type to gossip about anyone. Ruth knew that she could safely tell Liz that she was not going to be married, after all, and part of the reason why.

But perhaps, at the very back of her mind, there was

just the little hope that Liz might let fall a word in Oliver's hearing. Not that it would interest him, of course, or make the slightest difference to his own plans for the future. But she would like him to know that she was not marrying Daniel after all, yet she could not tell him herself!

"Best thing that you could do," Liz said in her direct way. "All very well in theory, that kind of marriage, Ruth. I must say he sounds a sensible and far-seeing person. Was it your idea that you should get married?" she added shrewdly.

"I suppose it was." Not even to Liz could she mention what had prompted her to think of marrying Daniel. No one must ever know that she had fallen such an easy victim to Oliver Manning after years of condemning him roundly for his amoral behaviour. "It seemed a good idea at the time," she said, a little wryly. "I'm really very fond of Daniel."

"Sorry for him, more likely. Or for yourself," Liz said shrewdly, the warmth of her genuine affection and concern removing all sting from the words. "It *is* unsettling when people are rushing into matrimony on all sides—and it's just the time of year when they will do it. I get the bug myself sometimes." She smiled at Ruth with understanding. "But it's a risky business even when two people love each other and if the love isn't there in the first place . . ." She shrugged expressively.

She had known Ruth for a long time and liked her very much. She admired her determination and her dedication but deplored the single-mindedness which had never allowed her to replace Neil. Ruth might suppose that she was not attractive to men. In reality, men were deterred by the chilly reserve and distrust, the armour

166

she wore about her heart. Only a very determined man with a very real interest would persevere in the attempt to break though the ice.

"I don't know that I've very much faith in love," Ruth said with an attempt at lightness.

"That's because you've been let down," Liz said bluntly. "But you musn't judge every man by Neil Plummer and it's about time you put him right out of your mind, Ruth. There are plenty of fish in the sea and most of them are much better catches, believe me!"

"All waiting to jump into my net, I suppose," Ruth said dryly. "I don't know that I want to catch any of your fish, Liz. There are better things in life than falling in love and hoping for wedding bells!"

"Not for a woman," Liz said firmly.

"Don't let the women's libbers hear you say so!"

Liz grinned. "I won't. Seriously, I am delighted that you and Daniel came to your senses. It's been worrying me, you know. He may be the nicest man in the world and my heart goes out to him. But, nice girl that you are, you'd have felt cheated eventually, Ruth," she said soberly. "You're a good nurse. You'll be a good wife and mother one day."

"And Mr Right is waiting just around the corner!" Ruth laughed. "You're a romantic, Liz!"

"Aren't we all?" she returned shrewdly. She turned at the sound of a familiar footstep. "Good afternoon, Mr Manning. We aren't ready for you, I'm afraid. I've been gossiping." Her plump, homely face wreathed in smiles, she went forward to meet him.

Oliver's glance slid past Liz to Ruth. Their eyes met and then she looked down at the list in her hand. He fancied that her eyes had hardened and pride rose in him fiercely. Damn the girl! She had turned his life upside down and would not give him one smile, one friendly word.

"Tearing some poor devil to shreds, I suppose," he said lightly, in response to Theatre Sister's greeting. She was so outgoing and friendly and warm-hearted that Ruth's defensive barrier seemed to strike more forcibly than ever. "I know I'm much too early. I wanted a word with my senior registrar and I was reliably informed that he was here."

"The bird has flown, I'm afraid. You'll find him in the pub at this hour. Do you care for some coffee? It is fresh." Observant Liz had noticed that brief exchange of glances and wondered. Ruth was suddenly absorbed in a totally unimportant piece of paper and Oliver Manning's light-hearted manner seemed strangely forced. She was intrigued.

"An excellent idea . . . thanks."

"I must get back to the ward," Ruth said abruptly, scarcely acknowledging the little nod that Oliver gave her. She laid the list on the desk. "I think that's correct, Sister Carter," she said briskly. "If you do have any queries just ring through to the ward."

"Now don't rush away, Ruth." Liz smiled, dismissing formality. "You aren't due back for fifteen minutes. Have some more coffee. Mr Manning will think that you don't care for his company."

Ruth could happily have strangled her friend in that moment. Liz was not usually so insensitive to atmosphere, she thought bitterly.

She managed a small smile. "Mr Manning knows that ward sisters are very busy people," she said coolly. "I can find a lot to do in a spare fifteen minutes before I'm officially due on duty."

"Mr Manning will hope to have the pleasure of your company another time," Oliver said, very dry.

Ruth sent him a swift glance that rebuked him for the sarcasm. Then she hurried out of the ante-room, wishing her heart would not leap in that foolish fashion for the mere sight of him. Heaven knew why she loved him when he had scarcely a pleasant word or a smile for her these days, she thought angrily.

Liz looked after her friend with a slightly calculating look in her warm, brown eyes. Ruth was too sweet-natured to snub anyone without very good reason—and that had been a decided and quite unmistakable rebuff! Liz knew that Ruth had never particularly liked Oliver Manning but she had always been pleasant to him in the past.

Suddenly it occurred to Liz that her friend had been around Theatres rather more than usual of late—and always at a time when Oliver Manning could reasonably be expected to appear on the scene. He was a very attractive man. Did Ruth feel drawn to him for all her former dislike of the surgeon? It would not be so surprising, Liz thought shrewdly. Perhaps that foolish engagement to her cousin had been a defensive action on Ruth's part, soon regretted.

Liz had never been in love but she was an acute observer of human nature and Ruth's behaviour was entirely in accord with the assumption that she had fallen in love with Oliver Manning, was far from ready to admit it and was terrified that he would find out how she felt about him.

"Ever tactful, our Ruth," she said brightly to cover the little awkwardness of the moment. "She knows how

169

seldom I have you to myself!''

Oliver smiled, a little absently, made some gallant reply in response to the flirtatious jest—and then changed the subject. He did not wish to talk about Ruth. There were times when he wished that he had never set eyes on her—and other times when the need for her was a physical ache.

In recent weeks, he had felt no interest towards other women. He did not want anyone but Ruth. He had taken Hilary Longhurst to a party, dined at her home, lunched with her one day when they chanced to meet at the hospital but it was all in the name of courtesy. He did not care much for her company. She was beautiful and charming and highly intelligent—and she irritated him.

Ruth had spoiled him for other women, he thought wryly, remembering her sweetness, her warmth, her generous giving, her youthful delight. She had enchanted him when she relaxed the reserve which had deceived him and every other man for so long. Who would know, watching the briskly efficient and coolly detached Sister Challis at work, that she could be so endearingly and appealingly feminine when she was away from Hartlake and all its associations? But he knew, he thought with a pang. He missed the side of her that he had known too briefly. She had allowed him a glimpse of the real Ruth and he had tumbled into love with her but was now kept so severely at a distance that it was a torment.

He seethed with impotent fury at the thought of her approaching marriage. He hated a man he did not even know with a fierce and jealous hatred. In the dark watches of the night, restless and troubled and without ease for the malaise of heart and mind and body, he devised ridiculous, schoolboyish schemes for preventing the wedding, for carrying her off, for forcing her to marry him. In the harsh light of each new day which inexorably brought her wedding nearer, he faced the unpalatable fact that there was nothing he could do to make Ruth love him.

He realised it was not the first time that a man had been disappointed in love. 'Men have died—but not for love . . .' Yet it seemed to Oliver that on the day when Ruth finally turned her back on the love and the life that he offered and married Cousin Daniel, something would die in him and never be born again. She was the only woman he would ever love. Without her, he had nothing. All his skill, all his success, all his achievement would turn to dust in his mouth. For a man was nothing without the woman he loved to walk through life with him, to give an incentive for working and striving towards the future. Better men than he had discovered that truth throughout the centuries. . .

It was Jessica Brook's last day at Hartlake and she was so excited, so radiantly happy, that it was pointless to expect any work from her, Ruth thought indulgently, working twice as hard herself to stifle the little pang of envy. Lucky Jessica had not made the mistake of caring for a man who cared nothing for her. Lester was kind and tender, a thoughtful and loving man. The kind of man who really merited a woman's lasting love—not like Oliver Manning with his careless disregard for the consequences when he encouraged a woman to love him!

Talk of Jessica's wedding was on everyone's lips. She was a popular girl and throughout the day the ward was visited by a number of people who came to wish her well, to bring her small gifts or hand over congratulatory cards signed by the staff of various wards and departments.

The eventful day was a tonic for the patients on Paterson, reminding them of the world outside the hospital walls, lifting them briefly out of the world of pain or anxiety or anguish. All the world loves a lover— and every woman delights in a wedding, thought Ruth, a little wistfully.

Oliver arrived for his teaching round, complete with a group of students, to find the ward in uproar as one of the more outspoken patients chafed the blushing bride on her approaching nuptials, much to the delight of the other patients and the juniors.

Jessica, a little drunk with excitement and surreptitious sherry, turned a glowing face to the consultant who surveyed her, smiling, having been forewarned by his senior registrar of the excitement on Paterson.

"I hope you mean to wish me happy, Mr Manning," she said gaily.

A little mischief glinted in the dark eyes. "I think it may well be my prerogative to kiss the bride," he returned smoothly.

Impulsively, she went to him and turned up her pretty face and, disregarding all the rules and regulations, Oliver kissed her lightly on the lips, cheered on by patients and students.

Ruth whisked out of the side ward, anger sparkling in her green eyes. She had overlooked a great deal during the day but this was too much!

"What is going on in my ward?" she demanded icily.

She sounded so like Sister Booth that her junior nurses hastily melted away to their neglected routines, the students shuffled their feet and looked away with a little guilt in their expressions and the patients lay back on their pillows and pretended to know nothing about anything.

Jessica smiled warmly, unabashed. "Mr Manning was just wishing me luck, Sister."

"In the nicest possible way," he supported her, his eyes twinkling. "For me, anyway."

Ruth glowered at him. "I think the whole world has suddenly gone mad over a mere wedding," she said furiously, sick with misery that Jessica should know the touch of his lips, the warmth of his smile.

"Your turn next week, Sister," Jessica said outrageously, winking at Oliver.

Ruth turned on her coldly. "That will do! Please go to my office and wait for me there and I suggest a cup of black coffee while you are waiting!" She turned back to Oliver. "Shall we begin the round, Mr Manning?" Her voice shook slightly but she met his dark eyes without flinching—and found that the warmth and humour of his response to Jessica still lingered. Her heart contracted with sudden longing.

"Certainly, Sister." He fell into step beside her as she moved towards the first of his patients. "I'm in your black books again," he said quietly so that only she could hear.

"Schoolboy behaviour!" she said scathingly, furious with him for that irresistible charm and with herself for loving him.

He smiled wryly. "A little laughter does no harm and sometimes does a great deal of good, Sister. The patients respond to a glimpse of humanity in us, you know." He moved forward to take the hand of his smiling patient. "Well, my dear, you're looking very much better to-day," he said in a gratified tone. "If you're doing as well

173

as you look we shall be sending you home within a few days. Chart, please, Sister . . ."

In passing it to him, their hands touched. Such a brief and meaningless physical contact but the shock of it travelled from head to toe of her slight body. She dragged her thoughts from the wistful memory of his gentle fingers at her cheek, against her lips, touching her breast like a lover and found him regarding her with a little frown in his dark eyes. "I'm sorry . . .?"

He repeated his request for a sphygmanometer. "I should like to check Mrs Arnold's blood pressure for myself, Sister."

"Yes, of course!" She beckoned to Phyllida Sims and sent her hurrying for the piece of equipment. "Is anything wrong, Mr Manning?" she asked, a little coldly.

He indicated the chart. "If this is correct then Mrs Arnold is no longer with us," he said dryly. "And, as you can see, she is very much alive and kicking."

She mentally consigned Phyllida Sims to the depths as the girl arrived with the sphygmanometer, managing to trip over an unwary student and collide with Ruth, knocking the pile of case histories out of her hands.

Ruth drew a deep breath, near to exploding. One of the students began to laugh—and stifled the sound in his throat as she looked at him with chips of ice in the green eyes. Phyllida bent down hastily to retrieve the files and cracked heads with an obliging student who bent down at exactly the same moment. Oliver choked and turned away hastily to look out of the window while the files were picked up and hastily marshalled into some semblance of order. Ruth looked at his shaking shoulders with acute dislike and called to Nurse Trevor who happened to be coming along the ward at that moment.

"Take over for me, Nurse," she said in a carefully-controlled tone. "It's time for Mrs Wilson's injection."

Oliver turned to watch her walk down the ward, head high and slender back stiff with affront. All desire to laugh abruptly left him. He turned to his group of students and quelled their murmur with one look, as he could when he chose, and went on with the round, ably assisted by Nurse Trevor. Ruth did not come back, busy about the ward and helped by a subdued Jessica Brook.

Later, on his way from the ward, he met Ruth in the corridor. He signalled to his students to continue without him and paused to speak to her. "It was funny, you know," he said gently.

His tone broke through her defences. He had not spoken to her so warmly for many a day. She looked at him ruefully. "That girl! Oh, if I could just bring Sister Booth back for a few days!"

"You're doing your best to take her place," he said, a little dry. "She would be proud of you."

A little colour stained her cheeks. She knew he did not mean the words as a compliment. "I am responsible for Paterson," she reminded him, sharp. "It seems to be turning into a bear-garden and it reflects on me."

"And I don't help?" His eyes were amused.

Her chin tilted. "Frankly, no!"

"I'll promise to be a model of propriety if that will please you," he told her lightly.

She threw him a sceptical glance. "I doubt if you are concerned with pleasing me," she retorted tartly. "But I should appreciate a little more decorum on my ward."

Oliver's eyes were thoughtful as he looked down at her small and carefully expressionless face. "Paterson won't be your responsibility for much longer. I think you will miss it very much, Ruth.''.

So he still did not know that her plans had changed, but even that apparently unconscious use of her name could not convince her that he cared if she went or stayed, married Daniel or not. After all, he had not been sufficiently interested to make enquiries, she thought wryly.

"I'm not leaving Hartlake," she said stiffly.

His heart quickened. "Oh . . .?"

"Not just yet, anyway," she qualified. Marriage might not take her from the work and the ward that she loved but she was beginning to feel that a change of venue, as many miles as possible from Oliver, might be a wise move.

For a moment, he had believed that she had changed her mind about marrying her cousin. For a moment, he had been near to catching her into his arms and to hell with decorum!

Then he had realised that she merely meant to go on working after marriage as did most girls. Well, there was no doubt that she was needed at Hartlake and it would be more rewarding for Ruth than dancing attendance on a disabled husband. At the same time, it would be hard for him to see her regularly and be reminded that she was forever out of reach.

"Very wise," he said warmly. "We can't really do without you, you know." He took refuge in that impersonal 'we' because he could not trust himself if he should venture on the personal. There was nothing to be gained by pushing himself on a woman who did not want him.

Her heart wrenched. If only she could believe that he would miss her if she did go, she thought bleakly. But there was some comfort in that little smile in his dark eyes, the first hint of friendliness in much too long. His tone was warm, too. She could almost believe that it held a hint of affection. Did he have memories as she did—or was she able to kiss and dismiss without regret?

"I owe you an apology," she said impulsively.

He raised an eyebrow. "An apology . . .?"

"I was very rude to you, I'm afraid." Her tone was cool, formal. It was not easy to conceal the yearning for the warm and intimate tenderness she had once known from this man.

"Were you?" He studied her thoughtfully, wondering at the unexpected offer of the olive-branch.

"Oh, don't make it difficult for me," she said with a rueful little smile. "You know I was beastly to you that day. You haven't forgiven me yet." And perhaps he never would, she thought bleakly, longing for a response he did not seem willing to give.

"You are mistaken," he said, brusque with the need to resist the temptation to kiss the small, sweet face. There was a very appealing sorrow in those expressive eyes.

She shook her head. "No, I'm not. Oliver, I am sorry. Please forgive me." Her smile was suddenly tremulous. "We used to be friends."

There was a very strange expression in his dark eyes as he looked down at her. "I don't think we've ever been friends," he said harshly. And it was true. Casual acquaintances had become lovers all in a moment and lovers could never be merely friends. No longer lovers, it seemed they had to turn into polite strangers, he thought bitterly.

Ruth paled. His words slapped her sharply in the face,

177

leaving her in no doubt how he felt about her these days. It was an unmistakable rebuff. Well, she was well served for the snubs she had given him, she thought miserably.

"Perhaps not," she agreed, courageously finding her voice. "I never liked you, certainly."

He smiled wryly. "No. Yet I always liked you, Ruth." He touched his long fingers to her pale cheek in a little caress. She trembled. "We could have enjoyed that day on the river, you know," he said softly and turned away.

"Oliver . . .!"

He paused, looked back, a question in his dark eyes.

She hesitated. Then she said: "Do you give second chances?"

He walked slowly back to her, hands thrust into the pockets of his white coat. He looked at her for a long moment. Then he smiled that slow, heart-stopping smile that caused so many of her juniors to sigh over Oliver Manning. "Only to people I like," he said quietly. "Tomorrow?"

He seemed to have an uncanny knack for knowing just when she was off duty—or was it possible that he made it his business to find out.

She nodded.

CHAPTER THIRTEEN

Perhaps it was wrong to be so happy at the thought of spending the day with another girl's fiancé. But it did not feel wrong and Ruth's heart lifted as the time drew near for Oliver's arrival.

She had so few memories of him to cherish. Why shouldn't she garner a few more before he went out of her life for ever? And how could she feel guilty when she did not believe that Oliver was at all in love with the girl he was going to marry. It was merely an advantageous match and Hilary Longhurst was just the kind of wife that a successful consultant should have.

No man could smile as Oliver had smiled, and touch her cheek in just that way if he loved someone else, Ruth told herself hopefully. And perhaps he would not marry Hilary Longhurst if she was to tell him how much she loved him.

It was just a dream, of course. But why shouldn't she dream for a while before she settled down to the harsh reality of a future without him?

The day she would have with Oliver would be filled with the stuff that dreams are made of, and she meant to capture every moment of it in treasured memories.

It was not difficult to be pretty for Oliver that morning. She felt pretty! Her hair, newly washed and sweetly scented, waved about the small face to curl on her shoulders. She would just be Ruth and leave starchy Sister Challis at home, she decided gaily.

It was a glorious morning, harbinger of a beautiful and memorable day, and her dress was just right—a summery print with its fashionable scooped neckline and flowing sleeves. Summer sandals with elegant high heels completed the ensemble.

She was ready just as the doorbell buzzed and she ran down the stairs with a new confidence in her step and in her smile to greet him. The house was very quiet. Those on day duty already were hard at work on the wards and those on night duty probably sound asleep. It was thoughtful of Oliver not to sound his car horn.

The welcome in her smile, in her shining eyes, banished all the doubts that had been troubling Oliver. He had been so sure that he would arrive to be told that she had changed her mind, that Daniel would not approve, that she did not want to encourage people to talk about their friendship.

"Come up for a few minutes. I thought you might like some coffee. It's percolating."

He followed her up the stairs and into the comfortable little room that held so many memories for him. "Thoughtful of you, Ruth. I'm sorry I'm late. Traffic's very heavy this morning."

She smiled at him. "I was so afraid you wouldn't come."

This was the Ruth he remembered—opening like a flower in the sun to reveal the inner core of warmth and sweetness and delightful candour that had bound him with swift enchantment. It was worth all the effort to penetrate that chilly armour to find the real and delightful Ruth.

180

He drank his coffee while she vanished into the bedroom to put the finishing touches to hair and face. He was standing by the window when she came out, looking down at the wilderness that passed for a garden and regretting such sordid surroundings for a lovely girl. He would like to whisk her away to a beautiful house filled with all that money could buy—preferably on a desert island a million miles from Cousin Daniel, he thought grimly.

Ruth knew the impulse to go to him, to put her arms about him, to kiss the lean cheek and bring a little glow to those dark eyes. She took a step towards him.

Oliver turned. "Ready . . .?"

Ruth was checked by something in his tone that set her at a slight distance. He settled her in the car with impersonal hands. He was certainly keeping her at arms' length, she realised, heart sinking. She ached for him to kiss her, to enfold her in those strong but tender arms, to want her with the fierce desire that found its swift echo in her own body. She gripped her hands tightly in her lap, resisting the impulse to reach out to him in a silent plea for some small sign, some gesture of affection, that would give her hope. But the whole day was before them and surely she would know the reassurance in his kiss before the day ended.

Oliver did not mention Daniel. Nor did she.

Ruth did not mention Hilary Longhurst. Nor did he.

But the shadow of Daniel stood between them whenever Oliver spoke to her, smiled at her. He owed the man nothing and yet found that he could not cheat on him. It was exquisite torment to be with Ruth and have to deny himself the sweet pleasure of her touch, her kiss, her nearness. He had to force himself to be grateful for these few hours, stolen from the man who was not yet her husband.

And the shadow of Hilary restrained Ruth from slipping her hand into his, saying his name with love and longing, inviting his kiss or the briefest of embraces. She loved him but he was going to marry that other girl and soon Hilary would lie in his arms and know the sweetness of his kiss, the ardour of his lovemaking—and he would sigh *darling* with that special note of tenderness in his tone.

Ruth blinked back the tears that threatened, determined to enjoy the day with him regardless of that beautiful shadow. She thrust Hilary Longhurst to the back of her mind and smiled at Oliver as they sat together in the prow of the pleasure boat as it made steady progress up-river to Richmond.

The sun was very hot but there was a little breeze on the river that cooled her face and arms. Everything delighted her: the sun shining on the water, the colourful barges, the swans, the busy river traffic, the flotsam and jetsam. Oliver observed the swift play of expressions across the sweet face as she gave herself to the enjoyment of the day. She was just a girl, he thought tenderly, a laughing, enchanting girl beneath the cool reserve and the carefully guarded maturity of the hospital sister. And she made him feel like a boy again. Youthful, optimistic, full of dreams. He loved her dearly.

The breeze whipped her bright hair across his face and she leaned back against him, laughing. He raised a hand to free her hair and swept it back from her face feeling her body tremble in swift response to his lingering touch, seeing the quickening in the lovely eyes. So she wanted him still, he thought, his heart leaping with sudden hope.

Had she been fighting it all these weeks because of some misguided sense of loyalty to Daniel who could not love her as she ought to be loved, could not give her all that she deserved?

Their eyes met. "I love you," he said, just as a passing pleasure boat of the same fleet sounded off its siren in salute to the company flag.

"What . . .?"

Oliver shook his head. Perhaps it was just as well that his words had been drowned by the siren. They would not alter her stubborn intention to marry Cousin Daniel.

"Oh, Oliver—this is fun!" she declared warmly as the passengers on one boat called and whistled across the narrow expanse of water to the people on the other, waving and cheering and enjoying the moment like the holidaymakers that most of them were.

He smiled.

She looked at him in sudden doubt. "You aren't enjoying it!"

"With you I'd enjoy anything, sweetheart," he told her, leaning forward to murmur the words into her ear so that she could not fail to hear him.

Warm, delighted colour swept into her small face. Like a child, just as endearing, she turned her head to rub her cheek against his own in a little, loving gesture. His hand tightened fiercely on her shoulder. She moved closer to him impulsively. "Hold me . . ."

No mistaking the plea, the need in those quiet words. Oliver put his arms about her and, drawing her into the curve of his body, he rested his cheek against her soft, shining hair. Damn Daniel. He needed these few moments of togetherness.

He heard her catch her breath. He was aware that her

183

heart was beating a little fast. He saw the swell of her breast beneath the thin dress and his body was urgent with sudden longing.

"I don't think this was such a good idea," he said wryly.

"Oh . . .?" She twisted in his arms to look into his eyes.

He saw a little hurt in her expressive face. "Do I have to spell it out for you?" He laid his hand along her soft cheek in the caress that was so particularly his own with its haunting tenderness. "Don't you know how much I want you, Ruth?"

Want, he said . . . and she felt a stab of disappointment, of dismay. He wanted her. It did not mean that he loved her. Oliver Manning had wanted so many girls with that sensual streak in his nature and they had all known his charm, his desire to please, his ardent and expert lovemaking. And when he ceased to want, he moved on to the next girl who chanced to catch his fickle fancy.

Well, she wanted him, too. There was no shame in wanting him when she loved him so much. Soon, he would be married and beyond her reach. For her rigid principles would never allow her to snatch her happiness at someone else's expense. There was so little time left for them to be together and so many memories to store up for the future.

Ruefully, with the future in mind, Ruth wondered if Sister Booth had known the brief joy of loving and being loved in the long-ago days before she settled for being one of the most efficient, most formidable and most memorable of ward sisters.

It was a perfect day. They lunched at a quaint little

pub that nestled beside the river and walked hand in hand along the towpath like lovers. In dreamy, contented mood, Ruth refused to think of anything but the magic of the moment. This was their day.

In the heat of the afternoon, they found a cool spot to sit—a grassy bank beneath a cluster of trees with the river flowing just feet away from where they sat. Oliver threw himself down and stretched at full length, closing his eyes and relaxing. Ruth was free to study him with her heart in her own eyes, loving him, admiring him. She was so proud that this man's skill as a surgeon could save lives, mend bodies, bring new hope to despairing human beings. She was so lucky to have known him as friend and lover, however briefly. He had enriched her life.

She sighed.

Without opening his eyes, Oliver reached to draw her to him as he lay on his back on the grass. Ruth resisted for a moment and then she leaned against him and brushed her lips against his lean cheek in the briefest of butterfly kisses. He smiled and his arm curved about her. She felt his lips on her hair, at her temple, very gentle.

Her heart swelled with sudden misery. For how could she bear to be without him and how foolish it had been to give in to the temptation of this day with him when it only served to remind her how soon he would be utterly lost to her.

She drew away from him. "What would Matron say if she could see me now!" she exclaimed, striving for lightness. "I'm sure this isn't approved behaviour for a ward sister."

"It has my approval," he said lazily. He opened his eyes and smiled at her. "You don't let your hair down often enough." He twined his fingers in the thick curls whose highlights reflected the sun. "We seem to have wasted a lot of time, Ruth," he said suddenly, a little wryly.

She understood him. "And now there's very little time left . . ."

She was free to love him. But he would soon have a wife. Pain rose in her so fiercely that it was impossible to keep back a choke of dismay.

Oliver was swiftly concerned. "*Darling* . . ." he said gently, with love. "What is it?"

She turned her head so that he should not see the tears, pretending to be interested in the antics of a couple of mallards at the water's edge. She could not allow herself to believe the tenderness in his tone. She did not dare to dream that real and lasting love inspired the endearment which caught at her heart.

It was too late to pretend that she did not care. Throughout the day, she had probably betrayed her love for him in a hundred ways. There was no sin in a loving that asked nothing in return. Besides, it would be a relief to admit the emotion that consumed her so fiercely that it ruled her days and her nights, her whole life.

She forced a little smile. "I'm jealous, Oliver. And it hurts . . ."

He was puzzled. He leaned to look into the lovely green eyes and found that they were no longer guarded so that she did not betray her feelings. His heart gave a tremendous bound. Did she love him, after all? To hell with Cousin Daniel and the rest of the world! She was his woman—for ever and ever, amen!

"You don't have to be jealous of anyone," he said quietly, a wealth of meaning in his deep voice. "Now or ever."

Ruth looked at him, doubtful. It meant too much to her to believe him too readily. She had to be sure. "What about Hilary?"

"Hilary!" He laughed, suddenly carefree, suddenly sure. "I don't even like the girl, my sweet!" His dark eyes smiled at her in swift, warm understanding. "I suppose the juniors have had me virtually married to her ever since Founder's Ball!"

"Engaged, anyway," she agreed, her heart soaring high as she realised how foolish it had been to take grapevine gossip for gospel. She should have trusted the feminine intuition which had insisted that something precious and lasting had leaped to life between them.

He reached for her hand and carried it to his lips. "Oh, my love," he said gently. "Is that why? All of it? Cousin Daniel, too?"

Ruth nodded. She leaned to kiss him with her heart on her lips. "I love you, Oliver," she told him. She could say it now without fear for her happiness, her peace of mind, her future. The look in his eyes assured her that she was loved.

"Then you certainly aren't going to marry anyone but me," he said firmly, his tone allowing no argument in the matter.

Ruth had been very well-trained. A nurse simply did not question the decisions of a senior surgeon. "No, Oliver," she said with a little sigh.

Her eyes shone with love and a great deal of trust. For she was very sure that his wife would never need to doubt his loyalty. His wife would be completely secure in his love. His wife would be the happiest and most fortunate woman in the world.

The surgeon, most unconventional of men, took the

sister into his arms and kissed her thoroughly without a care for the watching world.

And the world smiled with its usual indulgence for a pair of lovers . . .

<u>Two</u> more
Doctor Nurse Romances
to look out for this month

Mills & Boon Doctor Nurse Romances are proving
very popular indeed. So from this July on, we
publish an extra story each month. Stories will
range wide throughout the world of medicine —
from high-technology modern hospitals to the
lonely life of a nurse in a small rural community.
These are the other two titles for July.

ALL FOR CAROLINE
by Sarah Franklin

Megan Lacey takes up the job of speech therapist
simply as a way of avenging her cousin's broken
heart. But she makes a complete mess of things —
and loses her own heart into the bargain.

SOUTH ISLAND NURSE
by Belinda Dell

When both the Senior Medical Registrar, Sandy
Legrady, and the new house physician, Ian Dugall,
vie for her attention, Staff Nurse Erica Ryall is
forced to juggle with their affections . . .

Look out for these three great Doctor Nurse Romances coming next month

CHATEAU NURSE
by Jan Haye

After an attack of pneumonia, Nurse Hilary Hope jumps at the chance of doing some private nursing in France but does not expect her life to be turned upside down by the local devastating doctor there, Raoul de la Rue . . .

HOSPITAL IN THE MOUNTAINS
by Jean Evans

After a terrible car accident, Nurse Jill Sinclair accompanies her injured brother to an Austrian clinic where Baron von Reimer hopes to repair his injuries. But the Doctor Baron is such an attractive man that Jill soon finds herself in an impossible situation . . .

OVER THE GREEN MASK
by Lisa Cooper

An exciting new part of her life begins when Nurse Jennifer Turner first reports at the Princess Beatrice Hospital — but nothing works out as she'd dreamed after she meets handsome registrar, Nicholas Smythe.

On sale where you buy Mills & Boon romances.

The Mills & Boon rose is the rose of romance

Mills & Boon
Best Seller Romances

The very best of Mills & Boon Romances
brought back for those of you who missed
them when they were first published.

In July
we bring back the following four
great romantic titles.

FIRE AND ICE
by Janet Dailey

To fulfil the terms of her mother's will Alisa had to be
married before she was allowed to look after her young half-
sister, and Zachary Stuart was the only man prepared to
marry her. But Alisa's idea of marriage differed very much
from that of her new husband!

THE IMPOSSIBLE MARRIAGE
by Lilian Peake

Old Mrs. Dunlopp thought it was a splendid idea to leave her
large house and a lot of money to her great-nephew Grant Gard
and her young friend Beverley Redmund — on condition that
within six months they got married. There was one snag: the
two people concerned just couldn't stand each other!

WIND RIVER
by Margaret Way

Perri had come here to Coorain, in the Dead Heart of Australia,
to work, not to teeter on the brink of disaster with a man like
the cattle baron Gray Faulkner. But how could she avoid it?

THE GIRL AT GOLDENHAWK
by Violet Winspear

Jaine was used to taking back place to her glamorous cousin
Laraine, and as it seemed only natural to Laraine and her
mother that Jaine should take on the difficult task of explaining
to her cousin's wealthy suitor that she had changed her mind
about the marriage, Jaine nerved herself to meet the arrogant
Duque Pedro de Ros Zanto. But there was a surprise in store . . .

If you have difficulty in obtaining any of these books through
your local paperback retailer, write to:
Mills & Boon Reader Service
P.O. Box 236, Thornton Road, Croydon, Surrey CR9 3RU.